War on the High Seas

A World War II Novel

RICHARD G. HOLE

War on the High Seas
A World War II Novel

Richard G. Hole

World War II

@ Richard G. Hole, 2022

Cover: @Pixabay - lcarissimi, 2022

All rights reserved.

The total or partial reproduction of the work is prohibited without the express authorization of the copyright owner.

SUMMARY

It didn't take long to sink.

He did it before the corvette, part of whose structure still appeared above the water and the speed did not give all his men time to get out of the hull, which dragged them to the bottom of the ocean.

Dozens of boats now floated on the water.

Everyone, friend and foe, without distinction, rowed furiously towards the coast guard, but the latter was absorbed in his fight with the second submarine to be able to take care of them.

War on the High Seas is a story belonging to the World War II collection, a series of war novels developed in World War II

WAR ON THE HIGH SEAS

From the command deck of the Candell, James Hunter, captain of the Coast Guard, looked around.

As soon as the eye could reach, the huge convoy made up of fifty ships stretched out, which, following the Murmansk route, crossed the North Atlantic, at the request of that Russian port.

It was late afternoon and a light wind from the Greenland coast was rippling the surface of the ocean.

The coast guard, qualified for those tasks because of the shortage of warships, whose presence was necessary in other war theaters, bravely crossed the sector of the left side of the convoy that it had been responsible for watching.

James directed his binoculars into the distance and barely noticing his act began to whistle.

"Are you happy, Captain?" Asked Bruce Deut, the second in command.

"Frankly, yes," he replied. We have been half the trip without anything happening. Although it is too early to claim victory, I believe that this time we will be able to avoid those damned German submarines.

Deut leaned against the railing and blew smoke out of his black pipe.

"It's not too late for the dance," he said. Wait for us to approach the Norwegian shores. Those pirates have their nests there and they won't let us pass without making us move a little to the beat they touch us.

James nodded. Too well did he know that Deut's words were true. There was not a single convoy that could boast of having passed Norway, without having suffered casualties and they were not going to be the exception.

"I know," he replied, "but one always likes to think that the best is going to happen. And the best thing in this case would be for a regular storm to break out, forcing these marauders to remain in their shelters.

"Perhaps God will hear you and we will have a quiet journey," Deut replied.

He was slightly older than James, though less tall and stocky, and the blond beard that curled on his lower jaw contributed to a much more respectable appearance.

"I don't see anything," James said, lowering the binoculars.

Deut smiled humorously.

"I assure you that if they arrive, they will not pass their business card before," he replied.

For the remainder of the afternoon and night they sailed safely east, and by midmorning they spotted a ragged line, over which James directed his binoculars again.

"Norway in sight" he said to Deut who had just appeared at his side.

"And announcement of disgust," replied the latter.

However, the first warning to prepare for the fight was not received on board the "Candell" until the afternoon of that same day, when the rugged shores of Norway were already visible with some clarity.

The radio operator on board presented himself to James, holding a piece of paper, which he handed to his captain saying:

"It's from the convoy commander.

Hunter read the message. Commodore Crayton would announce that one of the scout ships had sighted an enemy submarine twenty miles to the south, and ordered him to detach from the convoy to investigate.

"Will we go alone?" Asked Deut.

"I don't know," James replied. But, if so, God help us, if several submarines have gathered to attack us.

He gave the appropriate orders and the little ship changed course, heading her fine bow to the south.

"The calm is over, Deut," he said.

"That's my opinion. And I think the one hundred and fifty men in the crew agree with us.

"I'm happy with such unanimity," James replied.

Something was going to happen. That was for sure. They still had no news that a German submarine had fled the battle when it had even a five percent chance of doing damage in its favor.

Ten minutes after leaving the convoy, when the silhouettes of the ships that made it up were still visible in the distance, James and Deut simultaneously averted their eyes from the sea, to move it to the sky, attracted by the noise that resonated in it.

"I eat the cannon, if it is not an airplane" said Deut.

He was gambling with all the advantages on his part. The device was perfectly visible in the distance. Its black mass stood out in the blue sky, drawing circles that it interrupted from time to time to launch itself on something in the water.

James caught it in the visible circle of his binoculars and announced:

"It is an RAF bomber. And, either I am very wrong, or it is attacking our submarine.

"Well, at least we will have help, if things go wrong," said Deut philosophically. Command to play zafarrancho?

"Yes.

The bells began to be heard in every corner of the gunboat and, obeying his call, all the men who made up the ship's crew ran to their posts.

As they advanced towards the place where the plane was fighting its rival, the watertight compartments were closed.

Those in charge of dropping the depth bombs, the gunners and the repair crews; they waited for the moment, their faces tense.

They were already a short distance from the point where the submersible should be, but they could not perceive the slightest trace of it. The bomber was heading south, but instead, two English corvettes accompanying them to protect the convoy were sailing at full speed to the right of the "Candell."

"Good news," James replied. Go ahead!

The submarine appeared to have been swallowed by the sea.

For over an hour they explored the surroundings to no avail. At last Deut said:

"Well. We lost it.

The coastguard turned on his haunches, heading toward the convoy at full throttle, but they had barely advanced half a knot when the lookouts gave a warning cry.

Petty Officer Cawston ran to James excitedly.

"A submarine on the surface, sir," he said. Behind us.

Again the bell rang calling for the crew to get out. James ordered to turn around and focused his binoculars on the submersible, but before the gunners had been able to fire, it submerged again.

However, that was not why the "Candell" left the field.

"Come on! Full throttle, "Hunter ordered.

In a few minutes they were in the place where the enemy had submerged.

"Begin to cast the charges," James ordered Deut.

The huge spherical grenades began to be projected by the catapult, raising huge jets as they hit the water.

A dozen of them were launched when the telegrapher approached James again, who was watching the maneuver from the command bridge.

The new message came from one of the English corvettes sailing at a junction in the Candell. Apparently he was attacking, together with his partner, another submarine that he had discovered with his detector device.

"It's already two" whispered James

Again he gave the order to turn the course and launched himself towards the place where both corvettes were launching depth charges in the hope of blowing up the submersible, joining them in the task.

Ten minutes later, when the darkness was almost complete, oil stains appeared between the foamy surface of the sea, removed by the charges.

"One less enemy," said Deut.

Not a single light had been turned on on the ship. James glanced at his watch, checking that it was nine at night. He still lingered around for a while looking for new enemies, and finally ordered the convoy to bow.

For ten minutes they sailed at full speed, while the joyous comments of the crew were heard, but the fight was not over yet, far from it.

Suddenly, a huge patch of white light seemed to emerge from the sea. James pressed his fingers against the bridge railing and exclaimed:

"Christ, Deut! They are attacking the convoy.

The light increased in intensity and volume, attracting the gazes of both sailors who were staring at it silently and sullenly.

Crashes of distant explosions began to reach the "Candell."

The booms of the cannon shots were mixed with the explosions of the torpedoes and the scene was illuminated by an oil tanker that was already burning and by the flares launched by the escort ships to better combat the attackers.

He ordered the machines to be put to maximum pressure and the two schooners were soon behind, but before the coast guard could reach the place of the fight another message was received from the convoy.

His fears were not without foundation. This one was being attacked by at least a dozen German submarines. One of the ships that comprised it had lagged behind and the order for the "Candell" was to take care of its protection.

"I don't like this at all," James muttered. I'd rather defend the convoy.

The foam of the ocean seemed to boil under the keel of the "Candell" when the course was changed again, and half an hour later they were in sight of the trailing ship, some six miles away from the convoy.

During the night they got closer to him. It must have suffered major breakdowns in one of its engines, as it was barely advancing at a third of its normal speed. James contacted his captain and together they continued their journey.

"What will happen up ahead?" Asked Deut.

They couldn't know. They were too far from the convoy even to hear the explosions of the projectiles. Only a faint light, rising over the surface of the ocean with ghostly appearances, told them that the hit ship, probably an oil tanker, was still burning.

Shortly before dawn they reached him, but by then the ship had sunk, though the water mixed with the oil still sizzled here and there.

James frowned. The slow speed imposed by the merchant ship had left them alone on the surface of the sea. The convoy had pulled away and they couldn't get a trace of it.

"What a ballot," he growled.

If the German submarines had been successful in their attack, it was possible that they would have moved away from the scene of the fight, satisfied with the results.

But in another case, perhaps they would have left some units exploring the sea. And they were there, accompanying that invalid of the seas ...

When she looked up at him, she saw a huge column of foam rise in the water next to the ship they escorted.

"A torpedo!" He muttered. We are ready!

Soon they were attacked as well. A second torpedo tore a wide crater in the water off the Candell's side, not hitting it for less than twenty yards.

All the staff remained at their posts, their faces tense.

Now James was sure that they would not be attacked by a submarine alone, but he was careful not to communicate his suspicions to others, so as not to demoralize them and only Deut was a participant in their fears.

"I figured it out," he replied with the greatest calm. " We have gotten into a bad step.

A new torpedo carved a furrow in the water, but passed behind the coast guard. At that moment the lookouts gave the voice of:

"Submarine to starboard!

There was the pirate of the seas, semi-submerged. In the uncertain light of dawn its turret and the wake it left behind were visible.

The "Candell" was on him with lightning speed. The submarine fled the combat and as soon as two cannon shots exploded beside it, it submerged.

But he was doomed. The Coast Guard hovered over him and the depth charges were re-planted.

A few minutes later, James smelled the oil, announcing that a second submarine had been sunk by the "Candell."

Could such luck be possible? He wondered.

It was the third submarine the Coast Guard had attacked in twelve hours and luck had not yet tired of showing them its face.

An hour later the sound detector indicated that another submersible was hovering around those places.

James was observing the oscillation of the instrument needle wounded by the hum of the submarine's engine when he heard a warning word above:

"Periscope!

Followed by Deut and the boatswain, he climbed the ladder at full speed, in time to see how he disappeared into the waters, leaving a whirlpool, as the only trace of his presence.

At his command the "Candell" was on top of him, spreading the sea of loads, although they could not know if they had sunk him or not.

"His helmet is very hard if he has managed to withstand that deluge of explosions" commented Deut.

The fifth submarine met them at noon. He was on the surface, about three miles away, and James turned to his second, exclaiming:

"It does not submerge. Do you think you are going to leave us behind?

When the "Candell" came towards him, he was convinced that it was not so when he saw it sink again and another depth charge seeding was made in the place where it disappeared from sight.

The weather, which had been calm until then, gave way to a hurricane wind in the middle of the afternoon, whistling through the coast guard gear, slowing down.

James sent for Deut and Cawston, announcing that they were close to the convoy.

"However, we will not be able to approach him until it is night," he said. If the last two subs have not been sunk, maybe they will follow us and we will put them on their track.

"Has the convoy stopped?" Asked Deut.

"Only a third of it, to pick up the crew of two ships that were damaged and had to be sunk. I just got a message from the Commodore.

"Then what do we do?

"Twisting the course from time to time, to mislead them.

When it began to get dark, he put the bow decisively towards the convoy, followed by the merchant ship, who did not leave his shelter.

"Look," Deut pointed out suddenly.

Again the white glow of a bonfire rose before his eyes.

"They keep attacking the convoy," James growled.

The sound detector announced the presence of a submarine dangerously close. James could see that barely five hundred yards separated him from him and the "Candell" turned around quickly to attack them with the spur.

"The cannons!" Thundered James.

As the coast guard raced through the waters, the gunners began their task.

It was clear that the submarine had been surprised as it rose to the surface. The observer had probably been watching the convoy without noticing the arrival of the coast guard and it was going to cost him dearly.

From the bridge, James was excited to see that it was a good-sized ship with a tall turret and heavy weaponry.

The crew members were caught in their binoculars. They moved rapidly, trying to line one of their guns toward the coast guard, all the while shouting warning.

"Those machine guns!" James exclaimed.

Half a dozen of them, heavy caliber, swept the deck of the submarine, from which they were only two hundred yards separated.

James watched the action with eyes bright with excitement. Beside him, Deut nervously chewed on his pipe.

"They are ours!" He said.

Suddenly Hunter felt a sharp pain in his back and right cheek and groaned. Deut turned to him and removed the pipe from his mouth, seeing the blood run down his superior's face.

James guessed she was trying to help him and clenched his teeth, trying to control himself.

"Quiet" he said in a serene voice. Give me your handkerchief.

Deut handed it to him and James wiped the blood from his face with it, then put it on the wound. Deut exclaimed excitedly:

"Get off the bridge, James.

"Now?" Asked this one. Do not even think about it...

He clenched his hands on the railing and watched the fight.

"Are they attacking us from behind, Deut?" He asked.

"Not that I know of.

"So what the hell has hurt me? My back feels like dozens of pins have been stuck in me.

Deut looked back. The shield of one of the cannons had fallen, detached by an enemy projectile and the splinters torn off by the shot were the ones that had wounded James.

The sub tried to turn as the "Candell" swooped down on it, but the Coast Guard's bow spur delivered a glancing blow, knocking half the ship's crew to the ground.

When they separated from the submarine the cannons fired on him again at point-blank range.

James felt an excruciating pain in his back, but he continued to give orders without leaving his post, feeling a thousand hot splinters burning his skin and flesh.

He forgot the pain as he watched his enemy shudder, shaken by the impact.

A light flashed on it for a second, then it was gone, and the men began to exit the sub, one by one, as the monster slowly sank.

"Pick up the castaways," he ordered.

The German sailors were swimming towards the coast guard, but before they could reach their side, they were swallowed up by the immense eddy produced by the sinking of the ship and disappeared absorbed by it.

James and the others didn't have much time to feel it.

The Candell was listing to port, and her captain soon learned that she had a fourteen-foot gap in her side, below the waterline, through which the water was gushing.

The wind had diminished in intensity, but still it raised great waves that put him in danger of shipwreck as they beat against his flanks.

James went down to the place where the fault had been located. Deut, who was following him, suddenly noticed the huge red spot on his back and shouted:

"You have to put yourself in the doctor's hands. You're going to bleed out.

"Leave me alone now!" was the answer.

Cawston had already started the bilge pumps, but despite their blazing speed, more water was coming in than they could pull out and the level began to rise.

It came to their ankle first, then their knees were damp from the brackish water of the Atlantic.

"There's nothing to do," the boatswain muttered.

Suddenly the light went out and the engines stopped. James swore.

"Poor 'Candell' has turned into a log," said Deut.

"And that you say it. I don't know if we can stay afloat for long.

The bilge pumps continued their work in the dark, handled by arm.

It was not the worst that the water continued to rise slowly, but the uncertainty. James knew very well that the fight continued and at any moment they could receive a torpedo that would end the sufferings of the brave little boat.

Fortunately for them it was already dark and visibility was zero. You wish not, Deut led him to his cabin when he noticed that his legs were bending, and James was stretched out on the bed face down.

Dr. Barnet stripped him of his clothes with a deft hand and examined the wound.

"It would take a powerful magnet to remove as many thorns as it has stuck in it," he said. However, I will try.

For half an hour, James spent the tortures of hell. The doctor poked at his wound with tweezers, and each piece of steel that he managed to remove cost the sailor a torrent of sweat.

Halfway through the task, he took the handkerchief he was biting from his mouth to ask Deut how the bilge maneuver was going.

"We have managed to plug part of the gap," he replied. We are working by candlelight, but I think we will manage to stay afloat.

At last, Barnet finished the task. When he had finished bandaging him, James, whose face was pale and disconcerted in the dim light of the candle that illuminated the cabin, sat on the edge of the bed.

The hours passed slowly and agonizingly, until the dawn light began to filter through the cabin window, making him look up.

And at that moment, like an omen of death, when they seemed to have triumphed, the voice of one of the men in the crew sounded above with tremolos of anguish, startling his heart.

"Ship in sight! It's coming to us!

James almost groaned.

She jumped to her feet, her lips pursed in determination. Now, more than ever, he was determined to fight aboard the Candell until his last breath, until his last missile, whoever it was.

Suddenly she felt her vision blur and her legs buckle.

"Barnet!" He called.

The doctor was already running towards him, holding him up. James put an arm around her shoulders and said hoarsely:

"Take me upstairs.

Barnet tried to protest. Thick drops of cold sweat beaded the sailor's forehead, whose gesture became more decisive.

"Don't say anything," he added. Above.

It was useless to argue with a man like this, possessed of an iron will despite his youth.

Barnet assumed that he was going through the ordeal of hell and did not explain where he could find the strength to ascend the iron ladder and climb to the bridge, with their help.

Once there, Deut appeared alongside them.

"Where is the ship?" Asked James.

Deut pointed him in a certain direction to starboard. James gazed darkly at the rapidly approaching black mass and ordered his subordinate:

"Let the artillery be ready to fire immediately.

As Deut relayed the order, James focused the binoculars on the ship, which was advancing toward them menacingly.

Anguish oppressed his chest. Would it be friend or foe? Would they have to fight again, in the condition of the "Candell"?

The other ship finally emerged from the wisps of mist that enveloped it, and its name, written on the stern in black letters, became perfectly visible to James.

"" Burza "" read. " Deut! "He shouted in glee. Don't shoot! It's the "Burza"! Signal him.

The flags flew in the air. James lowered the binoculars.

Without needing them, he was able to see the response signal being made to them from the Polish destroyer and that aroused a clamor of cheers from the crew of the battered Coast Guard.

"Hey, James!" Deut yelled from below. He comes to our aid.

The "Burza" was a Polish destroyer that assisted them in escorting convoys. In the evacuation of Dunkirk, the German aviation had left him without a bow, but, thanks to a superhuman effort of his crew and a miracle from Heaven that allowed him to stay afloat, he managed to reach an English port where they put a new bow.

Since then he has hunted German submarines with the same fury as if they were evil animals and had a service record worthy of appearing in the annals of the most ambitious captain of the navy.

The "Burza" maneuvered deftly, and was placed next to the Coast Guard and, with the help of his men, the damage could be repaired enough to go back to the United States.

The Polish ship escorted them for two days and two nights, until they were left in charge of a slender Canadian corvette, which protected it while the tugboat that was supposed to take them to the United States arrived.

At last the two American ships met in the middle of the ocean. By then James's wounds were on the mend, and as the brave tugboat's small figure loomed over the horizon, he couldn't help but gasp.

"Heavens, Deut! How brave they are! Look how daring to go out to sea in that shell ...

Neither he nor Deut were unaware that the Germanic submersibles came in their audacity to near the American coast. What's more, some of them had sailed upstream of the St. Lawrence River.

And yet the six or seven men on the tug had not hesitated to take such risks; aware of what a warship meant at the time.

The captain of the tugboat, an elderly man who smoked on deck as calmly as if he were strolling tourists on Lake Michigan, greeted them, waving his hand in the air.

Immediately a cable was thrown at them and the "Candell" said goodbye to the Canadian corvette, but before setting off, James presented his officers with three magnificent turkeys from the Coast Guard refrigerator.

The reception given to the "Candell" in the shipyards where it was to be repaired was worthy of a high-flying ship.

The entire crew received a month's leave and when they returned to Philadelphia the "Candell" was repaired, brand new and like new.

The gap had been plugged and the machines put in a good job. When James climbed back into it, he looked excitedly at the one hundred and fifty men who smirked at him.

"Boys," he told them. We are still on Hitler's blacklist and we have great things to do. I suppose that, like me, you are looking forward to seeing them again with your submarines, but for now this will not happen, because we have been assigned a new service that is more rested and closer to home, although not without risks.

There were murmurs of curiosity from his men and James smiled.

"Say it now," Deut urged him, who was at his side with the other officers.

"Starting tomorrow we will be patrolling the Atlantic coast, from New York to Halifax," said James.

Most of the crew welcomed the news with joy.

For several months they had been helping gigantic convoys to avoid the danger of the submarines, with serious risk for them, and a season of restful patrolling, always close to the coast, did not seem bad to them.

And so began a new life for the "Candell" and his men.

For three months they patrolled tirelessly along the coast, until all its ports, its inlets and its bends, kept no secret from them.

Boston, Providence, Portland, Nieuport, and Portsmouth were regularly visited by the "Candell," with no adventure worth mentioning during those ninety days.

The men were bored on board and James himself longed for the previous activity, which contrasted with that calm girl. It was what Cawston, the boatswain, said.

"They say that German submarines dare to get here. I'm not going to contradict them, but it seems that our presence has been enough to drive them away.

It would not take long for him to know that he was not right.

What happened was that the submersibles preferred to make their victims offshore and closer to their bases.

But when they realized the enormous protection that the ships of the formations enjoyed, there was no lack of bold captains who took as their objectives the coasts of America.

The "Candell" had a patrol mission to Cape Sable, Nova Scotia, where he exchanged impressions with the captain of the Canadian corvette that was patrolling the Canadian coast.

On one of these occasions, Henry Lawson, who was called the captain of the corvette, during which he let him know that a pair of German submarines had been seen at the mouth of the St. Lawrence River.

"It is not difficult to know what they are looking for" he said. Lake Ontario has become a huge shipyard where ten thousand-ton "Liberty" ships are built, which then reach the sea by river. There is no doubt that they are good prey.

"I think you are right," supported James. Anyway that's far north of our limit, but if you ever find yourself in a pinch, don't hesitate to give us a call.

Lawson thanked him for the offer. He was about the age of James.

His black hair, piercing eyes, and straight nose spoke of a Latin descent, probably French.

When he left the Candell, Deut shook his head and said:

"I like that boy. It is serene and calm and one of those who give something to do when they are pricked.

Lawson saluted from the boat carrying his corvette, the "Canadian," stopped at a quarter-knot distance, and the two sailors saluted back.

The Canadian sped away from them heading north. Deut, in turn, asked James:

"Let's go?

"There is no rush," he replied. We are going to explore the Bay of Fundy.

The deep bay opened, already in Canadian lands, between the mainland and the Nova Scotia peninsula. The "Candell" entered her, exploring her thoroughly for two days, finding nothing abnormal.

When they left it, James showed a desire to extend his normal journey north a bit.

So they climbed over the Nova Scotia little thing and passed Halifax, continuing their march north. Shortly after, at Sherbrooke, James gave the order to turn around.

They had barely advanced half a knot when Deut's eagle eyes fixed on a high-flying plane.

The crew members of the aircraft must have seen them too, as they descended at high speed and began to circle around the "Candell."

"He's Canadian," said James. " What will he want from us?

"Perhaps it warns us that we are in its waters" replied Deut.

"I do not think it's that.

It didn't take long for him to see that he was correct when the telegrapher handed him a message that he said he had just received from the plane. James read it and then handed it to Deut, asking:

"How about?

"Two submarines are attacking a Canadian corvette off Louisbourg" read Deut for the second time. Why don't you guys join in the fun?

"Could it be Lawson?" Asked James.

"We cannot refuse such a courteous invitation," James replied. On the other hand, it is the first opportunity to have fun that has been presented to us in three months. Let's go there.

The Candell hurtled northward at full throttle.

Barely a quarter of an hour later, the telegrapher came into contact with the corvette.

"It's the 'Canadian,'" he told James, who followed his manipulations with the greatest interest.

Let him know that we are coming to his aid.

The telegrapher asked for more details and they learned that the corvette had discovered a submarine crouched in the narrow arm of the sea between Newfoundland and the island of Cape Breton.

"The crew of the apparatus spoke of two submarines" recalled Deut.

"Well. We will find out soon.

The icy breeze from Newfoundland slashed their faces. The sea was calm, but the wisps of mist grew thicker as they approached the scene of the fight.

A few minutes later, the boom of the cannons reached his ears. By then, the corvette was launching urgent distress messages, showing that it was in dire straits.

"Quicker!" Roared James.

The Candell's machines were working at full throttle.

The ship was moving swiftly, as in its best days, but all speed was too slow for James' impatience.

Suddenly the "Canadian" messages became short three-letter signals, broadcast at regular intervals.

"SOS ... SOS ...

"Cawston," James roared through the internal phone, "can't you get more speed out of this damn boat?

"I'm sorry, sir," replied the boatswain uneasily. We're going to burst from one moment to the next.

"Even if that's the case, increase the pressure.

The "Candell" was flying. The booms of the cannon shots sounded more and more different, standing out most clearly against the noise of the air that swept the deck.

"The corvette no longer fires," said James. They are finishing her off with cannon shots.

Deut nodded. It must have been more than one submarine that was firing at the Canadian ship, for it to have been able to defeat it. Suddenly the watchman's voice tore through the air

"I see them, Captain," he exclaimed. Are two...

The gunners were at their posts, ready to use the cannons, and the depth-charge catapult servers were waiting only for the order to go into action.

Soon after, the show was visible to all.

The "Canadian" was slowly sinking into the cold waters of the ocean.

The plane flew over it and the submarines, but they kept it at bay with their anti-aircraft machine guns, at the same time that they tried to accelerate the sinking of the corvette with their deck guns.

"Fire, Deut!" James yelled. Try to aim well.

The "Candell" barrage was the first news to the enthusiastic U-boat crews of its presence behind their backs.

The projectiles raised jets of water next to one of them. Through the binoculars, James could see his crew members rushing off deck to dive.

It was necessary to hurry not to allow it.

As the Coast Guard advanced, its guns blared again and James gave a cry of joy when he saw that one of the submarines had been hit.

"The corvette is sinking," he muttered, "but at least we will avenge her.

The crew of the Canadian ship rushed to safety in the boats.

Meanwhile, the second submarine was slowly submerging and James gave the order to head towards it, without stopping firing at the other.

It didn't take long to sink. He did it before the corvette, part of whose structure still appeared above the water and the speed did not give all his men time to get out of the hull, which dragged them to the bottom of the ocean.

Dozens of boats now floated on the water. Everyone, friend and foe, without distinction, rowed furiously towards the coast guard, but the latter was absorbed in his fight with the second submarine to be able to take care of them.

The depth charges began to fall at the point where he had been moments before, that one. A dozen of them exploded a short distance from each other, before James ordered to go back to make a new seeding.

Meanwhile, the occupants of a pair of boats of the "Canadian", now permanently sunk, had managed to approach the "Candell" and were climbing up the sides of the coast guard, aided by its crew.

James scanned the surface of the sea. The wind increased in intensity by the second and he was not able to distinguish the expected oil stain on it. Deut was still dropping charges, but it was clear that he was perplexed and disoriented. At last he got on the bridge.

"That bastard has escaped us," he grumbled.

New castaways kept arriving at the Candell James saw from the bridge that Henry Lawson was one of them and was glad to his heart.

They were picking up the occupants of the only boat that had managed to detach from the sunken sub, when the lookout exclaimed:

"Periscope to port!

James glared there.

It was hard to believe, despite being true. The sub had deftly maneuvered under his nose, placing himself almost behind him, in a magnificent position to launch his torpedoes.

A white trail lengthened in the water toward the "Candell."

It was unheard of. Out of every one hundred submarines, ninety-nine would have rushed off, taking advantage of the confusion that followed both shipwrecks, but that madman insisted on fighting.

Well. He wouldn't be the one to stop it. Deut had also noticed the threatening line of foam and maneuvered deftly, avoiding the collision.

"Watch out for the second torpedo!" James yelled.

His warning was useless. The "Candell" stirred nimbly, but could not avoid the impact and a horrendous explosion shook him, as he was about to launch himself against the submersible.

James was thrown to the ground, but he scrambled to his feet and went down on deck.

The torpedo had torn off a chunk of the Candell's stern, through which the water was gushing.

Deut busied himself with the work of shrinking it at the same time that other men removed the wounded from that place. James returned to the bridge, gnashing his teeth in anger.

Lawson was there and commented:

"It's getting ugly.

"Now you'll see what's good," James muttered.

Obeying his orders, the "Candell" launched itself towards the place where the submarine was.

He did not fire again, perhaps thinking that the breach would be enough to sink the coast guard.

The device, for its part, flew very close to the water and from time to time fired its machine guns at it, indicating the location of the submarine.

"Loads!" James yelled.

The fearsome spheres began to fall again. Their explosions were so intense that the "Candell" jerked spasmodically without stopping.

It was impossible for the submersible to withstand so many explosions and, at last, when the air became hurricane, raising threatening waves, the oil stain that announced its destruction emerged on the surface.

Then James was able to take charge of the situation.

The Candell had suffered tremendous damage to the stern. In fact, all of it was ripped off by the roots, but fortunately Deut had managed to raise a wall with bags of cement up to above the waterline, taking advantage of the twisted irons.

"Bad," James muttered. The ship is overloaded.

In addition to his normal crew, he carried with them the hundred crew of the corvette, as well as a crew of German prisoners from the submarine, who remained on deck well guarded.

Hey, Lawson. You know these waters better than I do "he said. What is the nearest coast?

"Newfoundland," replied the Canadian. Port Aux Basques is not far. If we can get there ...

"If it weren't for this damn wind ...

The "Candell" was a very seaworthy ship, but in these conditions, mortally wounded and overloaded with men, it was very difficult for her to escape to safety.

James Hunter and Henry Lawson were two good sailors to try to fool themselves. With a single look they understood each other, but with another they decided to fight to the end.

It was still two hours before nightfall, but the fog hung over the coast guard, increasing the anguish of his agony.

The waves were piling up furiously, ramming his flanks, and the brave "Candell" bounced off his foamy backs like a rubber ball in the hands of mischievous boys.

On deck, the men clung to anywhere so as not to be dragged out to sea. Below, Deut and his men toiled toil, trying to remove a tiny part of the water that entered it from the ship.

Fortunately, the machines were responding firmly, and the "Candell" kept making its way north, hoping to reach the small port of Aux Basques.

In the cockpit on the bridge, James and Henry watched the gray masses of moving waves beat over the ship, melting into lace of foam.

James ordered them to look for Deut and, when he had him on the other end of the internal phone, asked him how things were going downstairs.

"Evil" replied Deut without palliative. " The waves have destroyed the wall of cement sacks three times. I think all is lost.

Hunter bit his lower lip, refusing to give up.

"Do you have any idea where we are?" Asked Deut.

"About six miles off the coast of Newfoundland," James replied.

"Sure? I thought the sea was pulling us in.

"Not. The machines respond well. Maybe we can get there.

Henry shook his head, obeying the impulse that the "Candell" would not sail again.

Half an hour later, James was also convinced that all efforts to prevent this from being the Coast Guard's last voyage were futile.

The gap not only gave way to the irrepressible fury of the ocean, but the waves, battling against the edges, enlarged it more and more, ripping the sacks of cement arranged by Deut, as well as the wooden planks and steel beams. of the structure.

"Nothing to do," said Deut. " Little by little we will be left without a boat.

The water was up to the men's knees and the "Candell" seemed to breathe like a mule up a hill with four men on it.

"He can't even with his soul anymore," Cawston pointed out.

That led James to order the telegrapher to start making calls for help.

"We will not advance anything," said Henry. All ships are sheltered in ports. If there are any outside of them, he will have enough to do with fending for himself.

"We will stay on the ship as long as I can hold out," James decided. It is dangerous to lower boats in this wind.

Henry agreed with him, but they both thought with anguish the moment they were forced to occupy the boats, despite all the dangers.

The wind had given way, but the fog was thickening.

"I'm still hoping ..." James started to say, but at that moment the lights went out, cutting him off.

"What's wrong, Cawston?" He asked through the tube.

"The water drowns the machines," replied the boatswain. " Hey, captain. It is useless to continue. The men start to get scared.

"It's okay. Let them come up on deck "ordered the young man. He turned to Henry and added, "It is preferable to leave the ship before it sinks." I don't want useless precipitation.

The machinists and repair crews were soon gathering on deck. The "Candell" was already a plaything of the waves, but the force of the wind was diminishing ostensibly, and the ocean was calming as if it were already sure of its prey.

The auxiliary oil lanterns were lit, and in their fading light James glanced over the group of dark-faced men.

"It's terrible," he said. The boats will be overloaded.

"If the storm subsides, we can reach the coast," said Deut.

James still waited a few minutes. The hurricane wind that had killed the "Candell" turned into an icy breeze, but the Coast Guard began to lie down to the right side. It was impossible to delay the game any longer.

The men lined up before the boats, which were descending to the sea, and each of them was occupied by twice as many as their safety allowed, sinking dangerously in the water.

"What shall we do with the prisoners?" Asked Deut.

James clenched his jaws.

"They are men like us and they have entrusted their lives to us," he said. They must be saved. Distribute them, Deut. One in each pot.

The US and Canadian sailors were not exactly happy with the new order. All of them were already tightening in an implausible way and the slightest weight diminished the possibilities of reaching the ground.

At last, they were detached from the side, until only one remained next to him.

"Down, Cawston. And you too, Deut, "James ordered. Henry, I was very pleased to meet you, "he said, holding out his hand to the Canadian.

"Aren't you coming?" Asked the bosun.

"No," James replied with integrity. " I will stay on board until ...

"That's crazy. I will not allow it, "exclaimed Deut.

James's eyes blazed.

"Down, I said. With you three, that boat carries ten more men. My weight would be enough to sink it.

"I'll stay with you," Henry decided.

"And I" said Deut.

"Me too," Cawston added.

"You cannot disobey me," he said. Down, I said.

Cawston hesitated. The "Candell" was bending for a moment. Voices of urgency came from below.

James reached under his raincoat and drew a pistol from its folds.

"I said come down," he said, brandishing it threateningly before the bosun's eyes.

Cawston hesitated. He flung a rebuke and straddled the deck.

"You, Deut. And you.

"I'm not leaving, even if it kills me," replied Henry Lawson. I am as much a captain as you.

"But not from this ship," roared James. Go away and don't worry about me. I have an inflatable boat and with it I'll try ...

"I'm sorry, but I'm staying." Henry's voice was firm as a rock.

The two men regarded each other antagonistically for a second. Anguished calls rang out again from below for them to hurry. James lowered the pistol, which carried Deut.

"Shoot if you want," he replied, "but I'm not leaving. Whatever becomes of you will be of me.

Hunter put the gun away.

"Well you know I can't do it," he said. Hey, those in the boat! Get away from here.

From the dark well below came Cawston's alarmed voice:

"And you?

"Go away, I said. In a few minutes it will be late.

The rhythmic strokes of the oars could be heard. Then the boatswain's voice came out of the darkness around the Candell, wishing:

"Good luck, Captain!

"Cawston ..." James muttered in a tremulous voice.

For ten months they had sailed together, running dangers and good times, which had established a deep friendship between them, to come to this ...

The Candell leaned further into the ocean, tired of fighting. The wind was still strong, but the sea was calmer and the boats would almost certainly be able to reach the mainland.

"Come on" Deut urged, "the ship will soon sink.

"Go get the inflatable boat," James replied. Let's fit all three.

Deut was already running on deck, which was inclined about thirty degrees. James saw him arrive at the casemate where the boat was and go out with him and a large pump to fill it with air.

In a few minutes they performed the operation. When they were about to launch the rescue contraption into the water, the "Candell" shook as if a gigantic fish had pulled him down.

"Hurry, Deut!" James exclaimed.

The ship finished leaning rather rapidly, while also bowing.

At last the water touched their feet. They put the boat down and Henry Lawson climbed into it.

Then James and Deut did, each on one side, and both vigorously wielded the paddles to get away from the wounded ship.

The boat was big enough to hold all three of them, but without any slack of any kind. Its wide edges, filled with air, were almost at the level of the water, supporting the onslaught of the waves. The two sailors rowed swiftly with their eyes fixed on the "Candell" ...

The brave Coast Guard screeched again, as if saying its last goodbye, and sank rapidly.

The waters of the sea parted to receive him and the oil lights went out, leaving everything plunged into absolute darkness.

However, the terrifying sound of the suction reached his ears and the airboat staggered dangerously on the edge of the whirlpool, forcing James and Deut to put all their strength in their hands.

At that moment, as if it had only blown to sink the coast guard, the wind ceased to moan as if by magic and the three men found themselves alone in the immense blackness of the Atlantic Ocean.

Deut sighed.

"Well," he said. Where are we headed?

There was not a single star to orient yourself by.

Henry was of the opinion that it was best to remain still where they were, waiting for the dawn light to allow them to head towards the coast, but James shook his head emphatically.

"That would be practically impossible," he claimed. " On the other hand, I am sure that I am not in the wrong direction. Paddle yourselves. I will lead.

Deut and Lawson obeyed him. Especially the first, he had already had more than once samples of the admirable skill of the young sailor to orient himself in the dark.

Powered by the oars, the inflatable boat moved with exasperating slowness. James seemed to know what he wanted, but Henry Lawson uneasily wondered if he was wrong.

"We have paid a heavy tribute for our victory," said Deut, still moving the oar.

"If it hadn't been for the storm, poor 'Candell' would have been saved," James replied.

For three hours they rowed without rest, although without making a great effort. James relieved them for some moments and let them rest for others, during which they consumed a few cigarettes. At the end of one of them, Henry Lawson expressed his opinion:

"It seems to me that we are circling, like a dog that wants to bite its tail In this darkness ... We should have already made landfall.

James didn't bother to contradict him. He had stopped smoking and was stiff, his head tilted to the right.

"Listen, sea lion," he finally replied. Do you know that noise?

"It's the hangover ..." said Deut. " The water crashing against the rocks.

"Exactly," James replied, and there was a note of triumph in his voice. What do you say now?

"I confess that I was wrong," acknowledged Henry.

"Where do you think we are?

"Near the San Pedro Islands" said the Canadian. " Or the pitfalls before them. If so, we will have to be careful.

"Well. I think we should continue.

Again the oars were grasped and the boat was propelled towards the place from which the sound of the waves crashing against the rocks came, which, little by little, became more distinct and precise.

"We're getting closer," James warned.

He tried to pierce the darkness with his eyes, but could see nothing but the phosphorescent foam that broke apart into fine glistening droplets.

He wished that the moon could break through the barrier of clouds that hid it, but his desire was not enough to achieve it.

"What do you know about those pitfalls, Henry?" He asked.

"They are dangerous," replied the Canadian. For me I would elude them. One mile further north, just behind them, is San Pedro Island. We could headed there.

"We will do it. The noise will serve as a guide.

They luffed slightly to the east. Soon after, the noise was to his left and the phosphorescent light caused by the tide began to fade into the distance.

At that moment James and Henry were rowing, Deut set his eyes somewhere in the distance. Then he turned to them and asked:

"You are tired?

"A little," replied Henry, "but I can still hold out for another half hour.

"So why the hell don't you row?

"Don't we row?" Asked James, puzzled. what do you mean?

"That we do not move from where we are," exclaimed Deut.

James proved he was right. Or rather, his partner was right, because, not only did they not advance an inch, but they seemed to go backwards.

"How weird!" James muttered.

"Weird? Nothing of that. We have gone to fall in a stream ", replied Henry". Now it will drag us south again and we will be very fortunate if we manage to avoid the pitfalls.

James and Deut were silent.

Henry was right. Either they managed to overcome their thrust or they would soon find themselves in front of the jagged edges of the San Pedro reefs.

"Come on, boys!" Encouraged Deut. Paddle hard.

James and Lawson stripped off their raincoats, which they left on the bottom of the boat, and rowed as hard as they could, but it was useless.

It was like wanting to fight a giant thousands of times stronger without weapons.

Deut relieved Henry, but his effort did not make the slightest change in the situation. Slowly but inexorably the current carried them towards the rocks.

James stopped moving.

"Do not send any more" he said to Deut. " It is useless and you will only get exhausted. Let it be what God wants.

The eyes of the three castaways rested on the rocks, as if they were possessed of a powerful magnet, which attracted them to death.

Little by little the phosphorescence of the water, divided into myriads of droplets, became more visible, and suddenly they were propelled forward.

The sound of the water hitting the rocks grew louder. The boat swiftly passed a tall rock, plunging into a tidal wave of motionless forms that rose low above the surface.

James tried to paddle him, and he succeeded for a long time, while Henry swallowed hard and Deut muttered curses more and more.

With each new push, the boat was suspended in the air, moving forward, between the rocks. As soon as one wave retired, it was replaced by another, which relieved it in its mission to play with the lives of the three men.

Suddenly his eyes fell on a huge rock that seemed to be moving towards him at breakneck speed.

"Watch out!" James yelled.

He pushed the oar forward to cushion the blow, but it splintered and the sailor was thrown out of the boat by the force of the impact.

At the same time, dozens of stony ridges dug into the boat, tearing the rubber and silk wrap, and the boat deflated in seconds through a couple of large gaps.

James swam vigorously toward the rock, yearning to catch up with it before another surge of the sea came.

The clothes were a hindrance, but he did not stop to shed them and gained the back of the stone, where there was relative calm.

The huge rock was less steep on that side. Drawing strength from weakness. James climbed onto it.

When he reached the top he was wheezing wearily, but considered himself happy to have saved his life, wondering what had become of his companions.

Sitting on the rock, he watched the stormy waters crashing their fury against the base, as if they wanted to destroy it.

"Deut!" He called. Deut ... Henry!

No one answered his call.

James gritted his teeth as he faced the night, cold, dark, and silent. Could it be that he was the only survivor of the three occupants of the boat?

What fate would have been the crews of the "Candell" and the "Canadian"? And the German prisoners?

Everything that happened seemed unreal to him. It was impossible for such a nightmare to be true. He would surely wake up soon.

The cold that penetrated him to the bones made him see crudely that he was not dreaming, but that he was in the flesh, alone and numb on a rock beaten by the sea.

Again he called:

"Deut! Henry!

He thought he heard a groan reaching him from a short distance away. James wondered if it was true or was it just another facet of the waters churning against the rocks, and repeated the call.

The moan reached his ears again, clearer and more distinct than before.

Who would it be? Deut or the Canadian? Whoever it was, it seemed to be in need of immediate help. Perhaps he had been injured when his body had been thrown against some rock, which he had desperately managed to grasp.

And he had to be there inactive, listening to those groans, which were like many other demands for help, without being able to come to the aid of the unfortunate one who was throwing them.

The thought of James crossed the idea, the crazy idea of jumping into the water and swimming to where the wounded man was, but he immediately dismissed it as impractical.

However, the moans brought him to life again and, driven by anxiety, James slid off the rock.

Coming into contact with the cold waters of the sea, he shed his boots, leaving them in a fissure in the reef, and resolutely stepped into the water and swam vigorously to the right.

A wave threw him out of his way, but he managed to grab onto a rock that barely jutted out of the seawater.

The moans were no longer heard. James made a horn with his left hand and called out to his companions, receiving in response a small voice that sounded a little later.

Taking advantage of the retreat of a wave, he swam again to a second step, where he called again.

The moan echoed in his ears again, clearer than before.

James fixed his eyes stubbornly on a group of small rocks that lay before him, barely thirty yards away, and crouched in his shelter, he watched the ebb of the sea before swimming swiftly towards it.

Touching one of the stones, he thought he saw something stir among the others.

With greater precautions, to avoid cuts with the edges of the rocks that surrounded him on all sides, he headed towards that point.

"Is it you, Deut?" He asked.

"No," replied a weak voice. " I'm ... Henry.

The Canadian was lying face down on a small plateau, little larger than his body, made up of dozens of small rocks against which the waves were foaming.

Each one that came, soaked her prostrate body more and more, but she did not have the strength to tear herself away from there.

James clambered onto the plateau, sitting on it, next to the sailor.

"Are you hurt?" He asked.

"Yes," Henry replied. In the head I must have ... lost a lot of blood.

"I can't see it now. Is it still bleeding?

"I think not.

James tried to make him more comfortable, leaning his head between his legs to protect you from the water with his back.

It was all she could do for him and he wished that dawn would come soon.

He was materially turned into an iceberg. His teeth were bumping against each other, driven by the shivering of the cold, and he felt an agonizing feeling that he couldn't bear the torture of the water crashing incessantly against his back.

Beside her, Henry exhaled wearily, but still had the strength to ask him.

"And Deut?

"I don't know what happened to him," James replied. It has probably died, washed away.

"I... I'm sorry.

"Don't talk, Henry. You are very weak.

The Canadian took one of his hands and squeezed it so lightly that James was alarmed.

And so two more hours passed, slow, silent, and cold.

James tried to cheer up his fighting partner, but even without seeing him, he could feel Henry Lawson weakening by the minute and he wondered if he could bear this ordeal.

At last, a slight grayish tinge hung over the ocean, as the waters stopped beating the rocks. James heaved an anxious sigh and stared at the source of the light, which turned white with exasperating slowness.

Henry opened his eyes and tried to smile, but his face, pale and impressively sharp, only drew a grimace that hinted at his true state to James.

As soon as he could see, which was not much, because of the mist that rose like a curtain from the cold, brackish waters, he could not make out the slightest trace of Deut.

Only the rocks, blackish, impressive and sad, stood between them and the open sea.

"How are you feeling, Henry?" He asked.

"Well ... now," replied the Canadian. It doesn't hurt ... nothing.

James did not reply. Too well he knew that this tranquility was a simple pause between pain and death.

He had seen many men die, whose sufferings ceased an hour or two before their life was extinguished, as if death, already certain of its prey, granted them that last grace of taking them away without pain.

Henry Lawson had a tremendous head injury, from which he must have been losing blood for a long time.

He had probably become numb after having managed to hoist himself between that handful of rocks and the sea water, beating against the wound, had prevented the blood from clotting.

The truth was that if help was not received, a fatal outcome was the only thing that could be expected.

The mist that enveloped them began to lift, giving way to greater clarity, but the sea was invisible even at a long distance. An hour later, Henry winced.

"Are you cold?" Asked James.

The Canadian did not reply. Maybe she hadn't heard him. It was the same anyway, because even if he knew he was chilling with the cold, he couldn't wrap him up any more than he already had.

Actually, except for his shirt and pants, James's other clothes fit around his body, although it was hard to tell if they provided any warmth or stole what little he could keep, due to how wet they were.

And the water kept hitting his back, which, despite the softness of the flogging, was beginning to hurt.

Desperate, he looked in all directions, seeing nothing but the sea and the mist, and he wondered how long he would have to be in such a situation, holding his companion's head between his knees.

"Hun ... ter" called Henry's weak voice.

James lowered his head to hers. The sailor's face had grown incredibly sharp and a translucent pallor covered his cheeks, as if the blood had drained from that body.

"What do you want?" He asked.

"In my ... warrior you will find some papers ... and among them the address of my sister ... Her name is Nell. Write to her or go see her ... and tell her that I died ... thinking about ... her.

"Come on, boy, who's talking about dying? James replied without conviction. We are on a very popular route and it will not take long for a boat to pick us up.

"But ... not me ... I know this is over ... I've stopped ... sailing ...

Again James tried to cheer him up, but Henry, after that effort, fell back into utter unconsciousness.

James gently laid his head on a stone and stood up. The sun, sad and whitish, was already lighting up the waters and the Yankee scanned the sea in all directions.

Towards the south, the bulk of a sailing ship glimpsed, towards the Strait of San Lorenzo, but it was too far away for its crew to perceive the signals it gave them, and it refrained from doing so.

"A ship, Henry," he said, looking back at his partner. It's coming this way.

Henry didn't answer. Alarmed, James leaned over him. His heart was no longer beating and his eyes, still open and full of marine nostalgia, settled on infinity, as if Henry had wanted to retain in them the last vision of his homeland.

James nearly burst into tears. A few more minutes and Henry might have been saved. He drew a deep sigh and said a short prayer, as a farewell to that fellow seaman whom he had known so little and whom he loved so much, nonetheless.

Then he remembered his assignment. What had he said his sister's name was? Nell; that was. Nell Lawson. Well. There would be time to collect your papers.

Then he remembered the ship and stood up again. As he did so, he noted his own weakness.

He was chilled and shaking from head to toe. The sun wasn't hot enough yet to shake that damn cold that made him shiver from his body, and James felt a sense of anguish in his chest and terrible pangs in his left side.

But the ship was approaching him. He was probably scouting the sea for them, if Cawston and the others had been saved and set the authorities in motion.

Soon after, James was able to perceive some details of its structure. It was a destroyer and it sailed slowly, probably exploring the surroundings.

He decided to swim towards the rock where he took refuge during the night, taking advantage of the calm of the sea, and, once at the top, he frantically waved his arms.

For a few minutes, the destroyer continued to sail parallel to him.

James swallowed in anguish, wondering if he was going to pass by, but could not help but groan with joy when he saw shortly after that it changed course and headed its bow towards the rocks.

Five minutes later, a launch emerged from the ship and its occupants rowed briskly toward it, skilfully skirting the reefs.

James was helped up into it by a young naval officer, who immediately threw a blanket around his shoulders and offered him a drink of brandy.

Then they went back to heading for the destroyer, but James said:

"There is a partner of yours on those rocks. Is dead.

Soon after, Henry Lawson's corpse was rescued as well. The officer stood respectfully before him and James noticed that his lips were trembling imperceptibly.

"Did you know him?" He asked.

"Yes," he replied hoarsely. " We were together at the Naval Academy. He was a great boy.

A pleasant laxity took hold of the American's muscles and nerves.

Once aboard the destroyer, he was taken to the infirmary, and the ship headed for Halifax. The ship's medic recognized James in detail and his face was grim as he turned to the captain.

"He has pneumonia" he said "; you will have to take good care of it.

"I leave it in your hands, doctor," replied the captain.

James's weak call brought them to the officer's bed.

"Captain," he said, Lawson commissioned me before he died to put me in contact with his sister. The signs are among his papers. Will you give them to me?

"There was no more.

He went to his cabin, where he had the documentation of the dead man, and returned shortly after with a note in his hand.

"Here they are," he said. Miss Nellie Lawson, 234 Kingston Street. In Montreal. Where do you keep your wallet?

James told him and the captain placed the note on it.

For five or six days, Hunter struggled with the disease, and his robust constitution, aided by science, overcame the crisis until he was fit to be transferred to Augusta.

Once there, he received a visit from his family and friends, and their presence revived the young man in such a way that four days later he asked the attending physician to discharge him.

"Is he so bad between us?" Replied the doctor with a smile. Sorry, Hunter, but it can't be. It has yet to wait.

That same day he wrote a long letter to Nellie Lawson, relating in detail the death of his brother in his arms and the answer was immediate, although not in the way that James expected.

It was three days after the letter was written, and James was telling himself that Nell might not reply to his letter.

He had little hope that he would, and he didn't really think about it too much. He had kept his promise and the girl was very willing to respond to her as she saw fit.

The group of friends who had come to see him had just left.

James was sitting in an armchair by the wide window overlooking the hospital garden, when the door opened again and Fleisch's freckled face appeared before him again, winking at him.

"There is a lady asking for you, James," he said. Boy, what a lady to spend convalescence! "He added smiling.

James frowned in puzzlement. Fleisch knew his sister well, so he mustn't refer to her.

Who could it be? He wondered.

Soon I was going to find out. Fleisch disappeared from sight to be replaced by the nurse; a pretty blonde, who didn't seem to take James's wooing badly.

"A lady wishes to see you, Captain," he said. Do you want it to happen?

"Who is it?

"Says her name is Nellie Lawson,

James put down the book he still held in his hands, driven by surprise.

"Of course I want to see it," he replied. Make it happen.

The nurse went to the door and opened it, gesturing invitingly to someone waiting outside, and Nell Lawson appeared in the doorway.

Fleisch was right, and he had expressed it with his peculiar levity of judgment.

Nellie Lawson was a woman capable of tempting a saint. Tall, undulating, with every curve in place and all well proportioned.

She dressed simply, but the black dress fit her perfectly and added a new charm to her bewildering personality and pretty figure.

Clearly, the girl had "glamor" and would not have gone unnoticed anywhere, not only by her figure, but also by that sad smile that spread her lips.

She was a brunette. Her hair was wisely combed and, by contrast, her fine white skin stood out like a smudge against the black color that dominated her figure.

Despite being brothers, he did not look like Henry at all. This was the impression that James picked up, as the young woman advanced to meet him.

James got to his feet. Nell stopped two steps from him and her lips trembled slightly. Then he stepped forward again and held out his hand.

"Sit down," he said, pointing to the other chair.

The girl did it before, demurely picking up the legs that she hid under her skirt and, without knowing why, James felt annoyed by that movement.

There was something strangely audacious about the young woman, even though she tried to hide it.

The nurse came out, leaving them alone. For a few seconds silence reigned in the room, until finally Nell said:

"I came as soon as I received your letter. Henry and I were alone in the world ...

She took a tissue out of her bag and wiped her eyes.

"You can imagine what it was like for me.

His voice was soft as velvet. Despite the occasion, James tried to imagine what it would be like to caress a man's ears.

"I understand," he replied. Sorry it took so long to write. I have also been quite serious.

" Oh, my God! You don't have to apologize. As you told me, Henry, my poor brother, died in your arms. Tell me how it was.

James did so, trying not to give his words too much emotion.

Nell listened to him with sustained attention. From time to time she would sigh or raise her handkerchief to her eyes, but it seemed to James that her grief was not as great as she was pretending to believe.

It seemed more like he was acting out a comedy.

Either way, he reached the end of his story, and, contrary to what he had expected, Nell Lawson did not make a big fuss when she heard how her brother's last minute had been.

She stood rigid and upright on the edge of the chair, her gaze fixed on the sky through the windowpanes.

When he turned them to James, they were expressing pain, impulsively leaned forward and nervously squeezed one of the young man's hands.

"Thank you!" She said, veiled with emotion. " Thank you! It must have been horrible for him poor Henry, but you ...

"It's not important. Forget it.

How can I forget him, when he was my brother?

James thought he didn't need to put so much feeling into his words.

He had done nothing for Henry Lawson, could do nothing except be by his side in his last moments.

He was afraid to ask Nell why she was hiding a pain she hardly felt, but he refrained from it, and he wanted her to get away from there to end this comedy.

Henry had spoken of her with a certain protective tone, as if his sister were younger than he and the idea of leaving her faced with the world frightened him.

But this woman seemed to be quite capable of supporting herself and having enough energy to lend to others.

At last Nell got to her feet, and James took another look at her tall stature, her domineering stance, and how little she looked like Henry.

He stood up and shook the long, slender hand she held out to him.

"Nellie ... Nell ..." he told himself. Even such a mild name did not fit that woman.

The name, especially the diminutive one, made one think of a pretty and feminine girl, with blond hair like gold and light and innocent eyes.

"When will you be discharged?" She asked.

"I do not know. In three or four days maybe, "James vaguely replied.

"Then maybe we'll meet again," Nell replied. I'm going to Boston and coming back here before I go back to Montreal.

"It will be my pleasure," he stated without conviction.

He had no interest in seeing her again. If he had been told that a woman like this was going to be interested in him to the point of pretending they would see each other again, he would have been, flattered and accepted without hesitation.

But she was Henry's sister, and it seemed a desecration to witness again the comedy of her feigned pain.

A lady like the one in front of him, whose hand he was still shaking, was ideal for going to night clubs, bathing with her on any lonely beach, going on excursions, or manning a sloop.

For the next three days, James Hunter couldn't get Nellie Lawson and her strange attitude out of his mind.

Several times he tried not to think about her, telling himself that perhaps the girl had felt obliged to visit him, although her relations with her brother were not what they should be.

Fleisch went to see him, and James realized from his questions that the redhead was very interested in Nell.

At last he was released and a car entered through the large door that gave access to the garden, stopping before him.

"Mr. Hunter," called a voice he hadn't been able to forget.

James didn't know whether to be happy or not, when he saw Nell Lawson's face leaning out of the window. The car was small and not very recent.

The young woman was driving it and there was no one else in it except for a dog dozing in the back seat.

The sailor came up to her, waving slightly, and Nell smiled:

"Was he leaving?" He asked.

"Yes. I have already been discharged.

"It was fortunate to be on time," she assured.

She was wearing the same black dress that she had seen him in the first time, but now she was wearing a pretty black hat which a white feather took away part of her sadness.

"Come up" he invited him ". I will take you where you want.

James was about to mumble an excuse, but before his brain dictated, his heart moved him toward the open door and settled next to Nell.

As the car started, he rebuked himself for having done it, obeying the powerful attraction that the woman exerted on him.

"Where do you want me to drop you off?" Asked Nell.

She was a right-handed driver and James couldn't take his eyes off her fine, manicured hands that handled the wheel with skill.

"Well ..." he hesitated. I was going to go to any hotel. Tomorrow I will leave for Boston. By the way, were you there?

"Yes. I have returned this morning, but I have to go back. We can make the journey together!

James replied affirmatively. He was extremely curious about Nellie, and he told himself that he might know what to expect from her on the journey.

Nell turned slightly to smile at him.

"Well. You still haven't told me which hotel you plan to go to.

"I have both one and the other," James replied.

"I'm staying at the Agnes," she hinted.

"There is no reason why I should not go to him too ... assuming they have a room

"I think there will be no problem with that," said Nell.

And that's how James found himself closer to her than he expected. But did he really want to be separated from her?

This question was asked in her room, concluding that Nellie Lawson was the most beautiful woman he had ever known, although her coldness and self-control took away some of her appeal.

He wanted to go for a walk, to breathe the fresh air of the sea and to tread the sand on the beach with his feet, but the walk would be more pleasant if someone accompanied him, and, almost without realizing it, he picked up the telephone receiver and he asked for communication with Nell's room.

It was she herself who got on the device. James asked him:

“Do you want to go out with me tonight?

"I would be delighted, James," she replied, "but ... under these circumstances ... Don't forget ...

"Do not worry about that. We would go for a walk on the beach.

“In that case, accepted.

James hung up the receiver satisfied, after agreeing on the time they would meet in the hotel lobby.

At nine o'clock, the sailor was in the hall, waiting for the young woman to come down.

When he did, he drew the gazes of the entire male element to his figure.

They both got into a taxi and James ordered the driver to take them to the port.

This was well lit by large spotlights and an intense activity was unfolding in it.

There were several merchants moored at the docks, which were loaded by hardworking workers, with the help of powerful cranes, and it was not difficult to deduce what they were transporting to them.

James told himself that soon another convoy would sail the seas, heading east, and sighed, wondering when he could embark again.

Soldiers armed with rifles surrounded the dock and did not allow the passage to the sectors where the war material was loaded.

James offered his arm to Nell and they both walked off to the beach. The night was beautiful and the silver moon kissed the waves that melted gently on the sand.

For a long time they watched the spectacle in fascination.

"Do you miss the sea?" He asked.

"Not by her side," James replied. Do you want us to sit down?

They did it on the sand. For a few minutes they had a trivial conversation, until, at last, Nell asked him again:

"Do you know when it will embark again?

"Well ... no," James replied. They may now grant me a short license and ...

"Where will he spend it?

"At my house, naturally. With my parents.

Would you like to visit Canada?

James turned to her.

"In ... your company?" He asked with intent.

Nell took a while to answer.

"Why not?" He said. It would be a great guide.

"I do not doubt it. Maybe I will decide to go.

Another pause, during which each one let their thoughts fly in totally opposite directions.

"Was he always in the Coast Guard?" Nell asked at last.

"No, no," James hastened to reply. I am what we could call a true fighter. This is the first comfortable position I've ever had ... and it wasn't that comfortable.

He went on to relate to her some events in which he had taken part, encouraged by the great attention she paid to his words.

When he told her about the last one, that memorable feat in which poor "Candell" had fought six submarines, Nell remarked:

"It must have been splendid. Do you want to go back ... to that?

"It is preferable to patullar without rest. New lands, emotions and women are known.

Nell giggled.

"Here you have met a new woman" he replied. What do you think of her?

James couldn't put into words what his opinion was, because he still hadn't gotten right to catalog Nell.

However, he opted for the easy way:

"Which is lovely," he replied.

He could have added that she was also overwhelming and dangerous, but he didn't, and Nell thanked him with a pout.

For another hour they sat on the beach. The waves began to approach and James decided it was time to head back to town.

They did so.

It was not until he found himself in the solitude of his room that he and Nell had never once spoken Henry's name all night, and he told himself that he had never known a case of coldness like that in relationships. between two brothers.

The trip to Boston created greater intimacy between them. James had stopped resisting, indulging in events, and readily accepted the details of trust and camaraderie from Nell Lawson.

She drove the car for the first part of the way, but then it was the sailor who took the wheel of her car. Shortly after, she took out cigarettes and offered him

"Do you want to smoke?

At his gesture of assent, he placed the cigarette to his lips, and after lighting it and stoking the fire with a long draw, he placed it in the mouth of his companion.

The light touch of her hand shook James, but she didn't seem to notice.

The cigarette was slightly stained with carmine, aromatic and slightly sticky.

Nell lit another for herself and leaned back in her seat. One of his legs brushed against James' and he did not separate from her.

"I am happy," he said. Rather. It would be if Henry hadn't died.

It seemed to James that it was in spite of this, but he did not express his thought, and replied:

"Then we would not have met.

"It's true. What are you going to do in Boston?

"Introduce myself to my bosses.

"And later?

"My near future depends on them. Will you be there for many days?

"Five or six. I dont know...

James refrained from asking her what reasons brought him to town, but she felt compelled to tell him.

"I have to choose several models of dresses, for my business in Montreal. Despite the war, women continue to worry about their clothes.

It was the first news he had about his activities.

They both stayed in the same hotel, not without having to travel three or four before finding a second-rate one, where they promised to provide rooms that night, and James went to the Marine Command.

From the Augusta hospital he had given his bosses a lengthy report about the event in which Henry Lawson lost his life, and now he was only very curious to know something about his new destiny.

He was sure that he would be sent again to command some warship.

That is why he looked puzzled at the head of the sector when he announced that he was assigned to his service, as a liaison officer between the Army and the Navy.

"But ... sir ... I would like, if it is not too much to ask, to return to the sea. Me...

"Maybe it won't be long, Hunter," was the reply, "but for now we need you here.

"The vice admiral came out from behind the table and put a hand on his shoulder." Don't think you're going to get bored ", he added. You will have more work than you want. I assure you.

James made a disappointed face, but was soon convinced that his superior was right.

The war raged day by day. The United States, turned into the arsenal of its allies, did not stop producing weapons at a dizzying rate and the ports were witnessing an unprecedented activity.

The sailor hardly had time to indulge in rest or recreation.

The shipment of the goods, the problems of the coast guard service, the relations with the armed forces, contained a thousand complex details and problems that had to be combined or solved in order for the machine to run smoothly and efficiently.

For the first few days, he could barely see Nell, although he spoke to her a few times on the phone.

When, at last, they managed to hold a long interview and he told her what his new position was, the young woman exclaimed:

"Magnificent!

James thought she thought they could be together this way, but Nell hardly thought about this.

The young sailor was devoted body and soul to her and her task.

The memory of Henry barely counted anymore and when it appeared to haunt him, James would apologize to himself that it was not his fault that Nell was too modern and independent.

One day, during which the work had been especially hard and intense, James collapsed into an armchair in his hotel room.

Nell was absent, but she was not long in coming, beaming with beauty and charm.

James looked at her, wondering when it would be time to part. Until then Nell had made no mention of it, but the sailor knew it had to come.

The young woman put the packages she was carrying on the bed and went towards him, kissing him.

"Tired?" He asked.

"A lot," James replied. I am a wreck. And more than that, what I have are a true desire to go out, to have a little fun.

"If you weren't so tired ...

"What?

"We could go somewhere tonight, dear. To dance for a while, for example.

James sat up in the chair.

"You don't know how much I would like him," he replied, "but it doesn't seem right to me, Henry being so recent.

Nell paused in her operation of shedding her hat and, holding it in hand, confronted James.

"Henry was my brother," he said, "but now I can confess that I felt his death as it can feel that of a relative with whom you hardly have any contact.

"You mean you and Henry weren't dealing?

"Since the war started I barely saw him a couple of times. And taking into account that since childhood our characters were totally different, you will understand that their absence cooled relationships in such a way. Please, Jim, don't make me tell you the reason for our disunity. Be satisfied with what I have told you.

That perhaps explained her lack of emotion at learning the details about Henry's death and her wanting to pretend to him, but James told herself again that it did not compel her to have paid him that visit in response to his letter.

"Good, Nell," he replied. Where we will go?

Her eyes gleamed.

"You are a charm" he kissed him again "Choose the site yourself.

"Is Parodies okay with you?

"By your side I will be delighted even in hell.

While they danced to the sound of the orchestra, James informed him that the next day he was to leave for Halifax in the company of the head of the sector.

"What are you going there for?" She asked without showing interest.

"A huge convoy is going to cross the Atlantic to bring aid to Russia," James replied, "and for the first time, it will be protected by US and Canadian warships jointly.

"How important is that?

"Not many. It is simply a matter of training Canadians in these matters. In Halifax we will set the number of warships from each nation that will protect the convoy.

"I will take the opportunity to go to Montreal. I'll be right back Jim

"Haven't you finished shopping yet?

"Actually, yes, but I must also attend to matters of the heart" she replied with a mischievous gesture.

James held her tighter and they continued dancing.

Two days later he left Boston, from which he was absent for almost a week. When he returned, Nell was already in town and asked him about the outcome of the conference.

"Great!" James replied. Your countrymen are really nice to deal with. There were no difficulties and everything was resolved in the first interview. Ships are concentrating on Halifax and other coastal ports.

"It must be exciting to travel in a convoy of those.

"Do not believe it. It's pretty boring.

"When will it come out?

"Within five or six days.

Nell deflected the conversation, but her eyes were fixed on the folder James had left on the table.

Soon after, he went into the bathroom and for a few minutes enjoyed his delights, humming a song.

When he came out again, Nell, dressed in a beautiful negligee, was smoking quietly, slumped in an armchair.

Five days later, a huge convoy, made up of a hundred merchant ships with a strong escort, plowed through the Atlantic waters, demanding the Murmansk route.

For a week, her bows sliced the waters in perfect order, protected by Yankee and Canadian destroyers and corvettes, according to the agreed plan, without the German submarines making an appearance.

The Canadian sailors were keen to cooperate, but they passed between Iceland and the Faroe Islands without the slightest setback.

All the crew began to believe that, by this time, they had managed to evade the attack of the fearsome German submersibles.

At the height of the twenty-fifth meridian, with scarcely a day left to turn the North Cape, to the northernmost point of Norway, a message was captured from the Russian navy, in which it was announced that several destroyers of this nationality were on their way to join forces. to the protection forces.

Two-thirds of the Yankee ships left the convoy heading south, to join another convoy leaving England for the United States on the high seas in search of more supplies.

This was the moment chosen by the Germans to attack.

For a few days before, the steel sharks, forming a veritable herd, had been lurking in their roosts, observing the movements of the convoy.

His refuges at Narvick and Vesteraalen were close by, and the operation looked most favorable to him.

Motionless and silent among the thousand islets of the Hammerfest region, the Germans watched the bulk of the protection units pass by.

As soon as they were out of sight to the south, they started at the highest speed of their engines, to fall on the convoy before the Russian units joined it.

The disaster had the characteristics of a true catastrophe.

The Canadian destroyers and corvettes fought heroically, but they were few in number and the crews were too inexperienced to defend themselves effectively against the combined attacks of a dozen submarines and fifty bombers.

More than thirty ships, including merchants and the Canadian navy, were sent to the bottom of the sea, along with their valuable cargo.

When the Russian destroyers arrived at the scene of the attack, it had already been consummated.

The torches of the burning ships still illuminated a bleak picture, in which hundreds and hundreds of men tried to get to safety in boats, boards torn by explosions or simply swimming.

As for the submarines, they disappeared from the theater of their feat, barely aware of the arrival of their most fearsome enemies, without leaving the slightest trace.

When this news reached Naval Headquarters in Boston, Vice Admiral Cramer convulsively clenched his fists and began pacing the office like a starving beast, under the grim gaze of half a dozen officers in his service.

At last he stopped before them, but did not speak at once.

"I don't understand," he murmured. I don't understand anything about what happened. How could they know when and where our ships would take off from the convoy?

He got no reply.

The same thing his officers were wondering about.

"The formation and route of the convoys was done in the greatest secrecy, to the point that not even the captains of the merchant ships used to know the way forward.

But it was clear that there was some infiltration or indiscretion on the part of one of the dozen people who knew the terms of the Halifax deal.

"Be that as it may," he added. There is no doubt that some group of spies have performed magnificently on this occasion. I will report to the authorities and henceforth we will take extraordinary precautions to prevent our plans from transcending the enemy.

The meeting lasted half an hour, but nothing could be made clear.

The Yankee officers swore and perjured that none of them had committed the slightest indiscretion, because they had not even told their friends or family about the convoy.

"Maybe it was the Canadians," one of them pointed out. Keep in mind that it was the first operation of this kind to be carried out.

"We will take that possibility into account, gentlemen" announced the Vice Admiral, "but meanwhile live with your eyes wide open and your lips tightly closed.

James returned to the hotel in a hell of a mood. Nell, who seemed to have the virtue of reading his mind like a book, guessed something was wrong with him and wondered.

"The worst has happened," he said. After painstakingly making all the preparations, he has suggested a real catastrophe. German submarines attacked the convoy leaving Halifax and have sunk more than thirty ships.

The girl gave an exclamation of surprise.

"The newspapers will give the news tomorrow," added James. Of course they will downplay the event, but it has been a blow to us

"Well, darling," she replied, "after all, it wasn't your fault,

"Not. Neither I nor any of the other officers involved in the convoy grouping, but the Vice Admiral seemed to see a suspect in each of us.

Nell diverted the conversation elsewhere.

"Are we going out tonight?" He asked.

"Damn if I feel like going anywhere," James replied. I think I'll go to bed without dinner, like when I was a kid and had a tantrum. Anything I ate would hurt me.

After the convoy mishap, others happened in the space of a few days.

They were perhaps insignificant things, but that added up, they came to worry the Boston marine authorities.

James was in his office examining some papers, relating to the effervescent underground activity of the enemy.

No matter how much he thought about it, he did not recall having committed any recklessness.

He was at this point in his thoughts when there was a discreet knock on his office door. James gave permission to enter and a sailor stood before him who told him that a woman who was waiting outside was requesting to see him.

"A woman?" James asked, intrigued. Was it his sister? Or maybe your mother? He doubted it because they would not have walked with such ceremony, but would have broken into the office.

Nell?

The best way to get out of doubt was to see his visitor and he said to the sailor:

"Well. Make it happen.

He waited for the lady to appear with real curiosity, standing behind the table. The sailor opened the door again, giving way to a woman whom James looked at carefully.

Was very young. Despite her black robes, and the total absence of makeup, it was hard to imagine that she was more than twenty years old.

The skin was smooth and white, and the face, oval and perfect, was crowned by beautiful brown hair. Everything about her radiated distinction, harmony and vitality.

The girl advanced determinedly towards him, outlining a smile not without sadness and the sailor thought that that smile reminded him of someone he had seen smile like that.

He quickly stepped out from behind the table and advanced on his visitor.

"Would you like to sit down, please?" He said, pointing to one of the chairs. How can I help you?

The girl sat down without taking her eyes off him. James did it in front of her and the girl asked him:

"Are you Captain Hunter?

His voice was fine and well timbred. James nodded, while replying:

"James Hunter, to serve you.

"I am Nell Lawson. Do you remember my brother?

She pulled back slightly as James was staring at her, his mouth hanging open in amazement.

And his perplexity knew no bounds when the sailor leaped to his feet and exclaimed:

"Good heavens! So who is the other one?

"No ... I don't understand what you mean," he replied.

James stopped in front of her, who was gazed into by blue, manly eyes, full of sternness.

"It is natural that I do not understand. Are you really Nellie Lawson?

"Of course," she replied surprised. " I can prove it to you, if you want.

She started to open her bag, but James cut her off with a gesture.

"No, it is not accurate," he said.

Now he was sure this was the real Nell. Not only because of the confidence with which she stated it, but also because of the resemblance to Lawson that she could read on his face.

The smile was mostly identical to that of the Canadian.

But then, who was the other one, the one who had been pretending to be Nell a fortnight before?

A suspicion nestled in his brain. A terrible suspicion that made him bite his lip.

"It is natural that I do not understand it ", he repeated at last, looking at his visitor, but with his mind set elsewhere". Very natural. And I am an asshole. Such an idiot will be difficult to find another.

He went to the window, followed by Nell's puzzled gaze, and stood for a few seconds looking out at the street.

Then he turned. The hospital scene was going to repeat itself, but now with the real Nell Lawson.

She had probably come to visit him to get news of her brother's last moments.

But at that moment he was in no position to think of anything other than the sinister scheme he had just discovered, to which he had collaborated with his idiocy.

"Miss Lawson," he said, facing the girl. I suppose you've come to see me to tell you some details about Henry's death, haven't you?

"For that and to meet him," replied the young woman with the greatest simplicity.

"How did it not come earlier?

"I work in Montreal in a military office" was the answer. I couldn't get permission until now. It took me a lot of work to find you.

"I understand," James muttered.

Her eyes were irresistible to him, but he must see Vice Admiral Cramer at once, as soon as possible, to repair the evil he had unconsciously caused.

Nell watched him, waiting. James leaned over to her and took her hands.

"I can't attend to her now," he said. I have something very urgent to do and you must accompany me.

"Me?" Nell's question exuded amazement. The girl stood up and said with some reserve ". I do not understand why I have to accompany him.

"We have to go see my boss," James replied. We have to solve something extremely important that also concerns you in an indirect way.

Nell showed in that moment that she had her own ideas and enough determination to stick with them.

"No," he replied. I don't have to go anywhere without knowing what to do.

Hunter looked at her slightly irritated. The girl was almost as tall as he, and now that he looked at her better, he understood beyond any doubt that she was indeed Henry's sister. Furthermore, a second deception on the same matter was difficult.

"Sit down," he said. Since I have no choice, I am going to tell you something.

She sat back intrigued. James did as well and began by saying:

"When Henry died, you commissioned me to contact you.

"Why didn't he do it?" She asked with some dryness. " The commissions of the dying are sacred.

James watched her silently.

"I wrote him a letter, giving him all kinds of details about his last moments. It also told you that the last thought of your brother was for you. Didn't you get it?

"No," Nell replied in a tremulous voice.

"I supposed. How did you find me then?

"The newspapers published his name. I made a point of meeting with you as soon as I could. Why? What's going on?

"Something very serious, Nell. Another woman is impersonating you.

"Because of me?" Asked the girl, intrigued. So that?

"To deceive me" he related what happened and the discovery that his arrival had just originated, reserving the details that he considered appropriate not to air too much, and ended up saying ": As you can see, they have used me like a doll.

A short silence followed his words. Nell was looking in a different way now, with more understanding in her eyes, mixed with a certain amount of sorrow.

"I'm sorry," he murmured. Do you ... want her?

"No," he replied fiercely. I've asked myself many times and the answer has always been negative, but now ... Christ! ... I would be able to kill her if I saw her again. And now, will you want to accompany me to see the Vice Admiral?

To her surprise, Nell shook her head.

"No," he said firmly. And before James's astonished look, he continued, "I'm going to tell you something that just occurred to me." And if after that you think that my idea is not a good one, I will go with you where I think my statement is necessary.

James materially drank his words, wondering what idea had gotten into that little head between eyebrows. Nell continued:

"This naturally hurts you, doesn't it?

"Much," he replied bitterly. Obviously, I can prove that I was deceived and they will not expel me from the Navy, much less will they shoot me, but I can now say goodbye to re-occupying positions of trust.

"Apart from that he will be the laughingstock of his teammates.

"That's how it is. Well. That is something that I have earned well for my stupidity.

He wondered why he trusted this girl so much, whom he had known only a few minutes before, and no answer occurred to him, except that she was Lawson's sister.

"But if you are the one who manages to catch her and her accomplices" because you undoubtedly have them ", your companions could not make fun of you and it will be somewhat in your favor.

James lifted his face to her, who stopped and smiled at him.

"What do you think of my idea?

"It's dangerous," he replied cautiously. " I do not mean the risks that I may take, but that they can realize something and disappear, with which my ignominy would be greater. No, I think we should bring it to the attention of the authorities. They have more means to discover the organization. By the way; It occurs to me that this must have ramifications in Canada. Otherwise, how was my letter intercepted?

"I don't know," Nell replied. His eyes flared and he added, "I don't think like you. With a little cunning he could strike a good blow to compensate him for the bitterness he is going through. What do you think the counterintelligence service will do? Well, simply ask them to continue the comedy until they have finished laying the network. Well. Well, that is precisely what I propose to you.

James considered the proposition.

A dull anger washed over him as he remembered that the fake Nell had played with him as she could have played with a poodle and he told himself that, indeed, he would like to make them understand that he was not as stupid as he seemed.

"Come on, make up your mind," Nell encouraged him. I would help you.

"In what way?

"Well... I don't know yet, but we will surely find a way to do it. Well, what do you think?

"I think I'll take your advice," proposed James. But we won't cover more than what we can bite into. I mean that if we encounter difficulties, I will report everything to my bosses.

"I like it that way," Nell replied, her eyes sparkling. " You will see how we will not fail. I will try to be close to you. For now, I'm going to stay at the same hotel.

"First, we must make sure that this woman does not know her.

"Can you show it to me?

"If at any time.

"The sooner the better.

"It's okay. I'll be with her in Cyrus in an hour. It's a bar on Concorde Street. You can take a look at it.

"Okay," Nell replied. In which hotel are you staying?

James told him.

"I'll call you on the phone later.

When Nell, after shaking his hand, left James's office, he considered the situation again and wondered if he had done well to accept the girl's suggestion.

She told herself that the best thing would have been to find out everything from Cramer, but gradually she grew excited again at the idea of making fake Nell swallow some of her own medicine.

At last, he picked up the receiver, summoning her to Cyrus for a little later.

That afternoon, Nell phoned him at the hotel saying that she did not know the woman posing as her, nor was it easy for her to identify her as Nell Lawson.

Anyway, it seemed better to James that the girl did not check into the hotel, but Nell insisted so much that there was no danger that she finally agreed, when she went to see him.

"It's okay. Do it, but with another name "he said.

They were both seated in his office at the Navy Command.

James decided in that moment that he liked Nell Lawson and spoke to his senses and to his heart in a way the other woman had never achieved.

"We have to live forewarned, especially you" said the girl. Do you think he will be able to pretend masterfully enough to deceive her?

"Don't worry about me," James replied.

From that moment he noticed the tutelage of Nell Lawson. The girl exercised a discreet vigilance over them.

Thus three more days passed, during which James made some observations regarding the false Nell, which ended up confirming his suspicions.

He and Nell met daily in his office, where they exchanged impressions that each day had a more intimate nuance.

In fact, both were attracted and each thought about the risk that the other could take.

One afternoon, Nell appeared in the office with sparkling eyes.

"Good news?" Asked James.

He sat next to her on the couch in the triplet. The girl replied:

"I don't really know, although I think I do. Do you know that your friend visits another man who lives in the same hotel?

"No," James replied, surprised.

"From what I have been able to observe it is not only a question of fellow espionage" she replied. There's ... something else. Love or something like that. And it occurred to me that we could take advantage of this circumstance.

"How?

Nell explained. James did not like the idea too much, but finally he allowed himself to be carried away by the girl's enthusiasm and agreed to act out the comedy that she proposed.

"When will you do it?

"Tonight. I'm on fire and wanting to get out of this mess. I think the only good thing about him is meeting you.

Nell smiled.

"I think Henry would have liked to hear you say that," he replied.

When the sailor returned to the hotel, the fake Nell was waiting for him, dressed to go out. To his question he replied that he was going to do some shopping.

Then he broke the news.

"Jim, dear," he said. We have little time to be together. I'll be back in Montreal in two or three days.

"But" he protested. " I thought you had arranged everything to stay in Boston indefinitely.

"And so it is, but from time to time I have to take a look at my business" she replied smiling. Why don't you come with me?

"To Montreal?

"Not. Now. I go shopping.

"I'm tired, Nell," James replied. And he had to put all his will in pronouncing this name ". I also expect a call ... And by the way, Nell, I didn't know you had a friend in this same hotel. You never told me anything.

He watched the effect his words had on the woman. He pursed his lips a little and paled slightly. However, he held her gaze steadily as he pulled on the gloves.

"A friend? You're wrong, Jim, "he replied.

"In any case, I am not the one who is. Read that.

From the pocket of his uniform jacket he took out a piece of paper which he handed to the woman, without telling her that he had written it himself, shortly before, disfiguring the handwriting.

"It was delivered to me downstairs this morning," he said as she learned the content of the false anonymous.

At last he raised his face, which was stamped with fury, towards James.

"It's a lie!" He replied fiercely. An infamous lie, don't you think?

"I think the same as you," James replied. "Good. It's not important.

She approached the sailor and impulsively kissed him.

"Thanks, Jim," he said. Thanks for trusting me.

He left leaving him alone.

Without the slightest hesitation, he began to make a systematic search of the woman's luggage.

Their disappointment was great when they did not find anything that would allow them to meet the other components of the organization.

Of course, the woman posing as Nell would have been careful not to leave the slightest trace that might help them.

They were cunning and knew very well that any carelessness could cost them their lives.

He picked up the phone and called Nell's room without getting an answer.

That was strange, considering that they had agreed that the girl would wait in her room for the result of the search.

He rang again, but the bell rang insistently, to no avail.

I'll wait a while, he told himself.

But restlessness dominated him. Without knowing why he sensed that the girl was in danger.

In vain she tried to calm herself and finally decided to call the "comptoir," asking if they had seen her leave.

"Yes, sir," replied the voice of the manager. She left a few minutes ago accompanied by a man.

"By a man?" Asked James. How weird! "He murmured.

The alarm sounded bugles in his brain, but the clerk's next words dispelled his suspicions,

"It was a friend of hers from Montreal, he said.

James hung up the receiver reassured on that point.

Surely Nell had had no choice but to get out. It did not occur to her that she had no need to give the comptoir clerk any explanation regarding the identity of the man with her.

In any case, she could have called him into his office or room to tell him.

He was smoking, deep in thought, when the bedroom door opened.

"Is that you, Nell?" He asked.

"Yes" was the answer. The woman posing as the girl appeared before him, greeting him.

"Hello dear.

He kissed her briefly and turned on more lights in the room.

"What were you doing?" He asked.

"Thinking," James replied. I look forward to this damn war over.

"We all have it, Jim," she replied. Hey, dear. I have something to tell you.

James was on guard. She asked him:

"Have you rested yet?

"Yes, Nell, what do you want?

"I wonder if you could join me tonight.

"Where?

"To a party" he cleared his throat and added ": You see. This afternoon I met some friends from Montreal. I had no idea they were here ... What are you looking at?

James was staring at her. I was wondering if one of those friends would not be the same one with whom Nell had left the hotel minutes before.

"I'm wondering if it is the one that anonymous was referring to," he replied.

He saw her make an effort to smile.

"Didn't we agree that you thought it was a lie?" He asked.

"Yes; But sometimes I can't help but think ... Well. You found those friends. What happened?

"They have organized a good party for tonight and they invited me to go. I did not commit myself firmly. If you want to accompany me, we will go. Otherwise...

"But, Nell, you know that you are very adept at doing what you like best. You can go alone ...

The alarm was screaming a warning at him. You had to be careful. Perhaps that comedian wanted to lead him into a trap.

Those friends he was talking about were probably his accomplices and he was going to get into the wolf's mouth.

"Well," he said to himself. After all, you were very interested in discovering them. Well now you can have the chance. Maybe they think you are mature enough to propose something ...

The truth was that he did not believe that this woman was going to get him into some trap.

They weren't, couldn't be, aware of the plan he and Nell were up to to find out. In any case they would limit themselves to meeting and chatting with the idiot who was playing their game.

"I don't want to go without you, Jim," replied the woman. If you don't come, I'll stay here.

"Would you really like to go?

"Go figure. It will be a good party.

"Where is?

"They have rented a chalet on the outskirts.

"Well. We'll go, "James decided.

She beamed. Try as he might, James couldn't find any hint of the triumph in her smile.

Before leaving, while the pretended Nellie Lawson put the finishing touches on your makeup, James was once again invaded by the strange sensation that he was walking towards a trap, but he was not willing to turn back.

He had been stupid to accept Nell's suggestion.

It was very clear that the two of them could do nothing against that organization made up of intelligent beings determined to everything.

However, he could still make a decision before it was too late, and, determined, he sat down at the table and wrote a few lines on a paper that he put in an envelope, on which he stamped the address of Vice Admiral Cramer.

She came out the moment he put it in his pocket.

"What is that?" He asked.

James carelessly lit a cigarette. If his suspicions were true, now, more than ever, he had to hide it.

"A letter for my mother" he said. Are you willing

"Yes, whenever you want.

Before leaving, he made sure he had the gun in his back pocket and calmly respected that end, closed the door and stood next to the woman, waiting for the elevator.

Once in the hall, he looked both ways, seeing no sign of Nell. He approached the comptoir and handed the letter to the manager.

"Kindly post it," he said, giving her a slight sign of intelligence.

"I will, sir," replied the clerk.

As he walked towards the exit accompanied by the woman, the clerk read the envelope:

To hand deliver, within an hour to Vice Admiral Cramer "he read.

The mariner's address was written below, and the clerk gave a hiss of astonishment, though he didn't know exactly what he was dealing with.

As soon as the couple got into the car that was waiting outside the hotel, another vehicle stood out from the row in which it was parked and followed them through the streets, which were quite crowded at that time.

The driver had to be very skilled, as he did not allow the car he was pursuing to get away from his, despite the fact that twice he was about to lose sight of him in the heavy traffic.

At last they found themselves on the Albany Highway, which skirted the windings of the Charles River, and the pursuer switched off his headlights, driving in the dark, even at the risk of crashing into a tree, to avoid being discovered.

A few minutes later, the car James was driving turned onto a back road at an indication from his companion.

"Will it take long?" Asked James.

"No," she replied. We are arriving.

At last, a chalet, rather a villa in its proportions, appeared before his eyes.

It was a Victorian-style building, surrounded by a garden, and presented a deplorable appearance, due to the modern air modifications made to its facade.

The garden gate was open and apparently no one was guarding it.

James had it on the tip of his tongue to ask the woman sitting next to him how she knew the location of the chalet so well, but although he was sure she had been there before that moment, he said nothing.

The garden gate closed silently behind him, without his noticing.

The man who drove it could not perceive the small car that at that moment stopped under the thick trees that lined the road, nor the man who jumped from it, approaching the house with stealthy movements.

There were four or five cars in front of it. James stopped the one who was driving next to them and, as he got out of it, commented:

"Wow. It seems that we have arrived last.

"No matter. They are trustworthy people.

The windows of the apartment were fully illuminated and a bright light came out through the cracks in the drawn curtains, turning the darkness into semi-darkness.

James and the woman advanced toward the house and she knocked on the door, which opened, as if they were waiting from within.

James and the girl passed into the lighted hall and the door closed behind them, giving James the impression that the trap in which he had just been imprisoned was closing.

And at that moment he was more than ever glad to have delivered the letter to Vice Admiral Cramer to the manager of the Amarillo Hotel.

The man who had opened it to them was a large, stocky fellow with a bulky skull, who vaguely reminded James of someone.

He was sure he had seen him, even if he couldn't pinpoint where.

"Hello, Master" she said. This is Captain Hunter. He is my friend, whom I already told you about.

"Nice to meet you" said Master, holding out his hand with a wide smile that almost erased the sailor's suspicions. " Do you want to go to the "living room"?

"Have they all arrived yet?

"Yes," Master replied.

The ten or twelve people, men and women, who were in the hall, turned toward the door as James and his companions appeared.

Decidedly, this had, indeed, the character of a party, in which, apparently, there was not going to be too much adherence to social norms.

The men were in shirt sleeves and they had cups or pieces of cake or cupcakes in their hands and each had managed to find a seat.

Soft music came from the terrace that overlooked the back of the garden, and the ensemble was pleasant and confidence inspiring.

But above all, James felt a kind of indefinable atmosphere, as if everyone in the room expected something to happen from one moment to the next.

"Guys, this is Hunter," Master said. You all know Nell, so there's no need to introduce her.

He had called her Nell.

This small detail convinced James that everyone was aware of his fake personality and there was no longer any doubt that he was surrounded by spies on all sides.

Spies simulating a joyous meeting of the unemployed, perhaps in case the police decided to intervene.

Well. They would not catch you off guard. If something was tried against him, he would try to buy time.

He was almost glad to think that he had been the one to lead the counterintelligence into the lair of spies, and he began to pretend that he was amusing himself while still keeping his eyes wide open.

Where would Nell be?

He was glad that he had been able to keep her away from all this, because the girl would not cease to be a hindrance if the moment came to have to resort to flight.

He danced a couple of pieces with the counterfeit Nell he knew and drank a few drinks, enough not to attract attention, but not enough to blur his clarity of judgment either.

The moment he returned back to the hall, Master approached him.

"Hunter, come with me" he said. There is a person waiting for you upstairs.

He was smiling good-natured when he said it.

James, without knowing why, was certain that these bandits would soon shed their mask of kindness.

He looked at the clock. It had been just half an hour since he had left the hotel.

Behind Master and followed by the woman, he climbed the carpeted staircase that led to the second floor. Once there, Master knocked on one of the doors and made an inviting gesture.

James made it through the entrance to a sumptuously furnished office, but had barely taken a few steps inside the room when he was pinned to the pavement.

"Nell!" He yelled.

His exclamation was confused with the noise of the door being closed and Master's ironic giggle.

"We were right, Lorna," he said. He does not deny that they know each other.

"109

James ground his teeth in fury at her stupidity, despite having the surprise factor as an excuse.

Nell was sitting in an armchair behind the desk in the office, pale as a corpse, and she couldn't find the strength to even smile at him.

The sailor turned to the door. The kindness was gone from Master's face, who was scowling at him.

Beside him, a man with skeletal thinness, high cheekbones, and lively eyes under a forehead that extended to the middle of the skull because of his baldness, also gazed at him, holding an automatic in his hands.

A little behind, Loma "had finally just found out his name," smiled at him sarcastically.

"Good," James said coldly. Now we play with the cards in sight. What are you planning to do?

"Maybe something is up to you," Master replied. Come on, Walter, explain ...

"Not yet," replied the skeletal individual. " Sit down. No, not there ", he said quickly, when he saw that James walked towards a chair located near a window". There. In front of her friend.

James did so.

"What's up, Nell?" He asked, smiling to encourage her. " It seems that we have been hunted like rabbits. How was yours?

"A man showed up in my hotel room, when I was waiting for your call. He told me that you were sending him to take me to Vice Admiral Cramer's office, where you were meeting. I thought it was a fool. As he passed through the lobby, he indicated that I should tell the manager that we were ... friends.

"I understand," James muttered. It was as easy as mine. Now if they tell me they pretend ...

"We want to know," Walter replied. You searched Lorna's luggage yesterday. She "pointed to Nell" has confessed that they have been interviewing for five days.

"Well. Well, you know everything, "replied James, smiling.

The skeleton's eyes steeled.

"You are very caustic, Hunter, but we are more so. What we want to know is who ordered her to follow the comedy, knowing that Lorna was posing as Nell Lawson. We want you to tell us what those Navy counterespionage agents know about us. Do you know why we are gathered here?

"I guess. You have collected candles and are preparing to flee, if things are as bad as you think.

"You are very clever, but it will not do you any good," Master threatened. I am going to leave him the face that neither his own mother will know him. I'm going to eat your liver.

He was furious at the ultimate failure of their plans and for not knowing what was being planned against them at the moment.

It was dangerous, but James couldn't resist teasing him.

"Sweet!" He said smiling.

Master snorted in rage and lunged at him. James rose to his feet, ready to repel the attack despite Walter's pistol, but Walter yelled:

"Still!

Master lowered his fists and ground his teeth in anger.

Lorna giggled briefly. She was sitting by the door, watching the scene with obvious interest, but James couldn't understand the reason for her apparent amusement.

"Will he speak or not?" Asked Walter.

"I suppose I will have no other choice," replied James, "but first I want to ask something. How was Nell's letter intercepted? How did they know that she had come?

"I know, Jim," replied the girl. It was Jane Barnet "and before the sailor's gesture of ignorance, she clarified": She is my roommate. She worked in the same office as me and we were like sisters. Apparently she is allied with ... with these ... "she did not utter any insults." I wrote to him from here telling him to send me some luggage, because I had found you and I was planning to spend more time than calculated. Imagine ... I've been a fool, a ...

"Don't worry, Nell. You could not know that she was a vulgar traitor to her country.

Master was enraged again. This guy was dangerous, but maybe not as dangerous as cold Walter.

"Jane has not betrayed anyone," he said. Her parents were German and she owed herself to her parents' homeland.

"Yes?" James asked slyly.

"Now you know everything and you can let go of what you know.

The sailor was silent.

It was clear that if he told these men that they had acted on their own, they would kill both of them so they could flee more freely.

Now everything depended on him. From him and Cramer. Success and life or failure and death depended on how quickly he put his men in motion.

He slowly got up from his chair and walked a few steps, followed by the threat of the pistol in Walter's hand.

As he put his hands in his trouser pockets, he felt behind the tension caused by his own weapon and was glad that he had not been searched.

"Freeze where it is!" Master threatened.

"Leave him," Lorna replied wryly. Maybe you need to focus.

Gain time. This was what he really needed. Never like then did he understand the value of minutes, even seconds.

"You are abominable," he snapped in the woman's face. " No one would be able to do what you have done.

"Don't tell me," she replied sarcastically. Is he going to give me a moralizing speech?

"Not. I suppose his parents would also be German.

"My parents and I. They brought me here when I was very young.

"Good, Hunter. We're waiting. "Walter's voice was cold and metallic.

"If I told you that other than Nell and me, no one knew about anything, you wouldn't believe me, would you?" James asked, facing the barrel of his pistol.

"Of course not. Do not come to us now with stories "Master replied in exasperation.

"Hush, Master. Is that true? "Asked Walter softly.

"Not. It is not. The agents of the counterintelligence service know everything, "James lied." They were the ones who ordered me to move on "he added viciously." Do you think you are stupid? They have them. Probably fifty of them will have followed us ...

Walter shook his head, clicking his tongue.

"He is lying. Lorna brought him right here, "he said.

"But we were under surveillance," James replied warmly. Someone must have seen us leave the hotel ...

"It's a lie," Master exploded. " Don't you understand, Walter? The first thing he said is the truth. They wanted to solve the matter by themselves. "He laughed unpleasantly, and added," Good, Hunter.

Here you have almost all the components of the organization. Why don't you take us and hand us over to the authorities tied side by side?

James glanced at Nell and, surreptitiously, at the clock. It was eleven o'clock at night, which meant that by now his letter would be reaching Cramer's hands.

Nell was very pale, but she was trying to stay calm. The young man thought the time had come to act. He did not know how, but the conversation was exhausted and the end, whatever it was, near.

"Anyway, the end of you two will be the same" said Walter coldly. They are a danger to us and they have to die. Then we will dissolve in the country until the storm has passed.

James took a few steps closer to Nell.

"Are they planning to kill us?" He asked.

Walter nodded.

"Come out," he said.

Lorna got to her feet, and Master strode to the door and opened it. Walter said again:

Come on, get out.

What I did not do now I would never do.

Nell gave a weak cry as she was pushed violently and fell to the ground.

At the same instant James crouched behind the table and drew the pistol.

Walter's projectile whizzed past his head and fired underneath in turn.

The little man grunted in pain and dropped the pistol as he felt hurt in the belly.

Master jumped out of the office, chased by a gunshot, and Lorna went to follow suit, but James yelled:

"Freeze where you are or I'll shoot you down!"

The woman raised her arms and turned to him with a fierce frown on her face.

Rushing footsteps began to be heard on the stairs.

James yelled:

"Close the door!

"Come and close it," she replied.

He had to risk being shot by Master, but it was essential that the door be closed before this mob of desperate men stormed the room.

James leaped from behind the table to the wall and ran alongside it, still pointing at Lorna.

Once at the door, he fired twice toward the stairs and had the satisfaction of hearing a cry of pain.

Then he slammed the door and pulled the bolt, pulling away from her.

A shout of warning from Nell was confused with the slamming doors that unloaded from outside on the wooden plank.

"Watch out, Jim!

James turned quickly.

Walter had managed to crawl a bit in his own blood and was holding the pistol again.

James went to pull the trigger, but at that moment some shots rang out and the projectiles pierced the wood with sharp clicks, ending Walter's action.

They were pulling the lock. Lorna was facing him on the other side of the door, her face grim.

"The tables have been turned, my dear," he said wryly. Why don't you use your sarcasm now?

"Do you think you can get out of here alive?

"Who doubts it? What I said was true. Listens.

He and Lorna held their ears out the window.

And, to James's surprise, commanding voices sounded outside, making him gasp.

Was it possible that it was Cramer?

He looked at the clock. No, he could not have set his men in motion in such a few minutes, still less have he got there.

Unless the letter had been delivered before the appointed time.

"What do you think?" He asked Lorna.

"You're a ... a ..." she exclaimed with sparkling eyes.

The men outside must have heard something unusual as well, for their agitated voices were no longer heard in the corridor.

"They are preparing to resist," James said to Nell, who had approached him. Can you handle a gun?

"A little," she replied. Henry taught me.

"Take that one" he pointed to Walter's. We have to disable the nice Lorna "Nell picked up the gun from the dead man not without some apprehension and James ordered again": Bring the cords of the curtains.

Shortly after, coinciding with the first shot, which announced that the spies were preparing to defend themselves to the end, Lorna launched completely harmless invective at them, tightly tied to a chair.

"What a tongue, my God, what a tongue!" Said James, scandalized. " And to think that there are women who can talk like that. Watch out, Lorna, my love! If you move violently you can knock down the chair.

The woman sparkled from her eyes, furious as a harpy.

For James that moment was sweet as nectar, realizing that, at last, he was going to be triumphant in the meeting. Nell approached him.

"Look at her," said the sailor. For several days we have been playing who's fooling who and at last ...

A booming voice from outside interrupted him. Whoever spoke did so through a loudspeaker

and his warning filled all areas of the house.

"Surrender! They are fenced off and have no chance of escape.

James frowned in surprise. He knew that voice.

"But, it's Sturges!" He exclaimed.

Things continued to take a favorable turn. Now it was only necessary that Cyrus Sturges had brought enough forces to storm the villa before its occupants managed to break into the office.

A volley was the response to Sturges' intimidation.

With her, the spies defined their attitude. They preferred to sell their lives dearly to surrender.

The shooting became general and streaks of light began to penetrate through the windows, coming from the headlights of the cars that surrounded the house on all sides.

"Nell, we have to do something," James said. Help me.

Between the two of them they placed some furniture behind the door, but the defenders of the house seemed to be very busy repelling the attack of their enemies, as they ignored them.

So half an hour passed, during which he was convinced that they had both forgotten.

"We have to do to help outsiders," he said.

The shots of the defenders of the chalet were less and less nourished, a sure sign that they were suffering casualties.

The most comfortable thing would have been to wait for the end of the fray in the relative safety of the office.

But the presence of Sturges there gave James some suspicions that were not at all pleasant, and he told himself that the greater his cooperation, the less his companions doubted him.

"I'm going out, Nell," he said. Take care of that witch.

"Don't do it, Jim. In a few minutes everything will be finished.

The sailor took her affectionately by both shoulders.

"I have to, Nell, don't you understand? My situation is very delicate. In the best of cases, I have been fooled and I have to cooperate as much as possible.

She swallowed hard and shook her head.

"I think you're right," he said. But, for God's sake, Jim, be careful.

He gently squeezed her hands and began to remove the furniture piled up behind the door noiselessly.

Then he unhooked the latch and slowly opened it.

The noise of the shots coming from below became more distinct.

Before jumping out of the office, James looked through the half-open door, but saw no one.

The smell of gunpowder hurt his nostrils as he cautiously poked his head out.

Immediately he was caught by the neck and thrown out and someone gave him a terrible shove that threw him against the railing of the stairs.

James lost the gun in the crash.

He stirred like a cat and was able to stare into Master's evil face.

The sailor rolled over as the mastodon pulled the trigger twice.

One of the projectiles sank into the pavement, but the other hit its target and James felt the lead bite into his right thigh.

"I'm going to kill you" roared the giant. I will kill you like a dog. I will fall, but you ...

He bent over James and lifted him upright with his left hand, throwing him against the wall.

The sailor tried to cling to it, but his strength failed him and he crashed into the wall with bestial force.

He groaned and slid along the wall until he was sitting on the floor.

Master raised the gun again and James closed his eyes, expecting the inevitable.

He heard three shots perfectly, but did not feel the slightest pain, and wondered how it was possible that Master had missed the shots at this distance.

Amid the mists that struggled to take over his brain, he saw him stagger and, in amazement, turned his head toward the office door.

Nell was there, holding Walter's pistol, with which he had fired. Master looked at her as surprised as he.

His strength must have been enormous, for, despite having conceded the three projectiles, he was still struggling to pick up the pistol that had fallen to the ground.

At last he succeeded and staggered before Nell, his left hand clutching his side.

"Shoot ... Nell!" James exclaimed hoarsely.

A kind of thunder came from the girl's hand, who closed her eyes at the same time.

Master grunted and took a few steps back. He tried to hold onto the stair railing, but could not do so, and rolled down it into the hall, where he lay still.

A man came out of one of the rooms at the sound of gunfire.

He was in his shirt sleeves, shaggy and dirty. Despair was in his eyes as he looked up and when he saw Nell rush towards James, he fired at her, but failed to reach her.

Then he ran upstairs. Nell shot him twice.

The second, the hammer fell into the void and the girl threw the pistol at him. The man ducked his head around her and continued up, pursing his lips furiously.

Nell snuggled against James, determined to protect him. His eyes fell on the sailor's pistol fallen by the railing and he ran towards it, before he managed to reach it the man reached up and pointed his gun at her.

"Freeze ...!" He roared.

As if her scream had been a signal, a roar of hell echoed through the hall.

The projectiles were shelled by the dozen, all at the same time.

Chunks of wood from the railing flew into the air, mixed with chips of plaster from the ceiling.

The man groaned and fell backward riddled with bullets. Nell matched his moan with a swoon.

"Yes," replied the vice-admiral irritably. " Of course I received your letter, but what you should have done was brought your discovery to the attention of Sturges or me. It would have been easier for everyone.

"I'm sorry Mr. I had to be the one to unmask them. It was my duty, since I was fooled like a Chinese.

"That will help you to be more careful in the future," said Sturges. " By the way. You didn't need to have run out of handkerchiefs to point your way to Vice Admiral Cramer. I already had all the members of the organization located. An agent of mine followed you and that Lorna out of the hotel.

James laughed softly. He was lying on the bed in a large room in the Navy Hospital, and Cramer and Sturges sat next to him.

"What are you laughing at?" Asked the first.

"I told Walter, I mean the skeletal individual whose body was found in the office, I told him that a counterintelligence agent had followed me and he didn't want to believe me.

"Good, Hunter," Cramer said, standing up. "I'm glad everything went well. Do you know that we came to fear for a moment that you were in league with these scoundrels?

"Me?" Asked James in amazement. For what reason should he be?

"For the love of Lorna, naturally.

"It wasn't love that I felt for her," James replied. Now I know.

"And I suppose it was Nell Lawson who made you notice the difference, right?

"Indeed," James smiled. Hey, Sturges, did any of them get away?

"No one. We charged twelve good pieces, most of which we were looking for. And the agents from Canada got under way at the same time as us. You see, Hunter, you exposed yourself to no avail.

"Do you believe?" Asked the latter.

"Good," Sturges conceded. Perhaps it was not entirely useless. At least he has cleared his name of suspicion.

The two men left, but the door did not close. Nell appeared in it, closing it behind her, and advanced on James.

"How are you feeling?" He asked.

"Very good, Nell... you were very brave to face that beast. Do you know that I owe you my life?

She blushed intensely.

"What else could I do, Jim?" He asked.

"You are admirable," he affirmed, taking her hand. " But you don't know what you've done. You have saved my life and now you will have to keep it ... always.

He looked at her eyes.

"It will be a very pleasant occupation, Jim," she replied, her eyes sparkling with happiness.

"I'm glad you think so. By the way, you once told me that promises made to the dying were sacred. Do you know that your brother made me promise to marry you?

Nell laughed.

"It is probably a lie, but, anyway, I am willing to carry out his last will.

"Well, he didn't say it, but I'm sure he did. Nell, we have to try to strengthen good neighborly relations between our countries, don't you think?

She affirm with her head.

"Well then, could you give me a little advance.

He raised his head to her, offering his lips to her.

Nell Lawson leaned down slightly and brushed them with her mouth, but she had fallen into the trap.

Jim's strong arms wrapped around his neck, but he didn't have to strain to make the kiss go on forever.

END

www.ingramcontent.com/pod-product-compliance
Lightning Source LLC
Chambersburg PA
CBHW061355160726

47995CB00001B/323